SENSUAL SOUNDS

A ROCKSTAR MÉNAGE

MICHELLE LOVE

CONTENTS

About the Author   vii
Sign Up to Receive Free E-Books and Audiobook Codes.   ix

Blurb   1
1. Chapter One   3
2. Chapter Two   8
3. Chapter Three   13
4. Chapter Four   18
5. Chapter Five   23
6. Chapter Six   28
7. Chapter Seven   33
8. Chapter Eight   37
9. Chapter Nine   42
10. Chapter Ten   47
11. Chapter Eleven   52
12. Chapter Twelve   57
13. Chapter Thirteen   61
14. Chapter Fourteen   68
15. Chapter Fifteen   73
16. Chapter Sixteen   80
17. Chapter Seventeen   85
18. Chapter Eighteen   91
19. Chapter Nineteen   96
20. Chapter Twenty   101
21. Chapter Twenty-One   105
22. Chapter Twenty Two   111
23. Chapter Twenty-Three   115
24. Chapter Twenty-Four   121
25. Chapter Twenty-Five   126
26. Chapter Twenty-Six   131
27. Chapter Twenty-Seven   136
28. Chapter Twenty-Eight   141
29. Chapter Twenty-Nine   147

30. Chapter Thirty	151
Sign Up to Receive Free E-Books and Audiobook Codes.	157
Other Books By This Author	159
About the Author	161

Made in "The United States" by:

Michelle Love

© Copyright 2020 – Michelle Love

ISBN: 978-1-64808-165-1

ALL RIGHTS RESERVED. No part of this publication may be reproduced or transmitted in any form whatsoever, electronic, or mechanical, including photocopying, recording, or by any informational storage or retrieval system without express written, dated and signed permission from the author

Table of Contents

❀ Created with Vellum

ABOUT THE AUTHOR

Mrs. Love writes about smart, sexy women and the hot alpha billionaires who love them. She has found her own happily ever after with her dream husband and adorable 4 year old. Currently, Michelle is hard at work on the next book in the series, and trying to stay off the Internet.
"Thank you for supporting an indie author. Anything you can do, whether it be writing a review, or even simply telling a fellow reader that you enjoyed this. Thanks

facebook.com/HotAndSteamyRomance

SIGN UP TO RECEIVE FREE E-BOOKS AND AUDIOBOOK CODES.

Would you like to read **The Unexpected Nanny, Dirty Little Virgin** and **other romance books** for **free?**

You can sign up to receive these free e-books and audiobooks by typing this link into your browser:

https://www.steamyromance.info/free-books-and-audiobooks-hot-and-steamy/

Or this one:

https://www.steamyromance.info/the-unexpected-nanny-free/

BLURB

Lust. Lies. Double lives

The rock and roll industry is full of people who are looking out for themselves, and willing to do anything to rise to the top. Those who are in the thick of it know what it's like to stab someone in the back, and they know what it's like to be stabbed. For five brothers, the rise to fame has been filled with trouble and hardship, but they have persevered. Now they're at the top of their game and the top of the charts too. Nothing can stand in their way. Their album is going platinum, they have more fans than they know what to do with, and money is pouring in faster than they can spend it. In short, life is perfect.
When a call from back home comes in and ruins their plans, they have no choice but to make some changes. They might be dragged back to their hometown, but nothing prepares them for what awaits.
Nikki thinks she's finally made it in life. She has fought her way through college and landed the job of her dreams.
But when her client makes a request she feels is impossible to

grant, she doesn't know if she's going to be able to keep her promise.

But a vow to a dying man is still a vow, and she's going to do all she can to make it happen.

Her promise becomes even more difficult to navigate when five hunky men from her past are involved. She's thrown into a life she never thought she would live, and faced with decisions she never thought she would have to make.

Who will she pick? The tall, dark, and mysterious one? The one who makes her doubt herself but drives her wild? Or the old flame that quickly grows into a blazing fire?

Go harder. Be better. Rise above

All my life, I've had to strive to be better than I am. Good enough is never good enough. I always feel like I have to do something better, or I'm never going to be happy.

I dedicate my life to helping others, and I've resigned myself to the fact that I am meant to put my own needs aside to make sure the people around me are getting what they need.

That's when they return. The brothers. All five of them. When I was younger I had a crush on one of them. At another time I had a crush on two. Then all of them. I thought I'd forgotten about them, but here they are, back again, and wanting me this time.

I thought I had my life together. I thought I was strong. But when any one of them touches me, I feel my knees go weak. How can I choose just one of them?

I can't.

CHAPTER ONE

Tommy

"Listen, Joe, I know you're pumped, but we just got back. Why not give us a couple of days before we pack up our things and head out again?" I try to sound casual about it, but I'm hoping he knows I'm dead serious. I really don't want to swing another European tour right now, and I can sense that's what he's about to suggest.

"I know, but think about it, Tommy. You guys are riding high on life right now. Sold-out stadiums, new fans in every city, and did I mention that it's a great way to increase sales on the previous albums?"

I wince, knowing he's right. This is the first project that's reached this level of success, and the more we push it on the public, the more likely we'll be to pull some of our other work out of the ditch.

"But you have to factor in the cost of us getting over there, not to mention the cost of hotels, and all the other shit I just don't want to deal with right now," I reply. I hear an exasperated sigh come through the phone, and though I can hear a smile in his voice, I sense he's forcing the charm.

"Profit my friend. Profit. You aren't looking at the big picture right now, and I really wish you would. Do you realize the kind of profit you could be looking at right now if you guys suck it up for a few months and give the public what they want? You don't want to be a one-hit wonder." I feel tension growing in my chest at the accusation.

Sure, we've had a tough time getting our foot in the door as a band, but that doesn't mean that our latest hit is going to throw us into one-hit-wonder status. Our sound is good. Our lyrics are good. Our rhythms are excellent. No one is talking about this song as being anything but great.

"We've got to sleep sometime, Joe." I try a different angle. Before he has the chance to respond, my phone chirps and I glance down. I don't recognize the number, but there's something vaguely familiar about it. My first response is to ignore it and continue my conversation with Joe, but there's something else compelling me to answer.

"Hello?" I say at last, after putting Joe on hold.

"Yes, may I speak to Mr. Bridges, please?" The voice coming through the line sounds professional. I'm curious how she knows my name, but I'm still drawing a complete blank.

"Yes, this is Tommy Bridges. Can I help you?" I'm beginning to suspect she must be some sort of telemarketer, and I'm preparing to tell her off.

"This is Cindy Davis from Hope Hospital and Psychiatric Center. How are you doing today?" she asks.

"Fine, thanks." I keep my reply short and sweet.

"I am calling in regards to your father. Unfortunately, while the cancer is still in stage three, it has metastasized once more, and he's in the hospital." I feel a twinge in the pit of my stomach and my heart skips a beat.

"What the fuck's wrong? Is he dying?" I ask abruptly. I no longer feel the need to be polite. Though neither I, nor any of my brothers, have had a good relationship with our father for years, the thought of him passing is enough to make me feel anxious.

"I'm not able to share much more information on the phone, but he did put in a request that I reach you and tell you he would like to visit as soon as possible." She is speaking in a low, gentle voice, and I know it's merely the training that has her doing so. I curse under my breath once more.

"A visit? What the fuck does he mean by that? It doesn't sound like he's going to be going anywhere anytime soon," I snap.

"I think he means for you to come here. He wants to see you and all your brothers. So far you're the only one I've been able to reach." I can hear an almost accusatory tone in her voice, but I shrug it off.

"We live a bit of an unconventional lifestyle, so we have to be careful about the information we make public." I don't want to tell her there's another reason all my brothers had their telephone numbers changed, and that was mainly so they didn't have to hear from our father.

"Right." She drags out the word, and I can sense she sees right through my lie.

"Anyway, thank you for getting a hold of me with the update. I'll be certain to spread the news on to my brothers, and we'll be in touch," I lie. I'm not entirely sure I'm going to say anything at all at this point. What is there to say? That our father is still fighting cancer and he's probably going to die from it one day?

We've known that already for years. The prognosis hasn't changed anything in all this time.

"I would encourage you to be timely about it," she says. I don't give her time to continue with a lecture, thank her once more, and hang up the phone. As I hit the button to return to my call with Joe, however, I can't shake the guilt that's quickly growing in the back of my mind.

"Thought I'd lost you," Joe jokes when I get back on the line.

"It was something with my father. I guess he's not doing so hot," I say, my voice more absentminded than I intend for it to be.

"Oh shit, I'm sorry to hear that. He dying?" Joe asks. These days, he's gotten to be as callous about the situation as the rest of us.

"I'm not exactly sure how bad he is. He wants to see us," I say, my mind clearly still on other things.

"Are you going to?" Joe prompts.

"I mean, shouldn't we? He's our fucking dad, after all. If he kicks the bucket, I think we'd all regret not getting to see him one more time," I snap. I'm not sure why I'm feeling so emotional about this, but I don't want to talk about it.

"Well, why don't we pencil it into the schedule?" Joe suggests.

"The fuck do you mean?" I ask.

"I mean, let's take the tour stateside instead of going over to Europe. I bet you'll get some attention going back home, small town though it is. Not to mention you can get seeing your father out of the way, and hopefully increase sales some more." I can hear he's already planning the trip without me, and I sigh.

I know he's right, and the way he's presented the idea makes it even shittier of me to turn him down now. The truth is, it would be a great way to continue with the promotion of the album while also getting to see our father.

For all I know, it might be the last time.

"You still there?" Joe's voice comes through the phone, and I realize I haven't answered in a few moments.

"Yeah. Listen, you work out the details like you always do. I'm going to get a hold of the guys. They're going to need as much warning as they can get." Joe laughs, though I'm only half-joking, and I hang up the phone.

I sigh as I drop into a chair and drag my hand over my eyes. It's been years since we've been home, and just as long since any of us have had any true contact with our father.

Regardless of the circumstances, this wasn't going to be a pleasant trip by any means. As far as I'm concerned, the sooner we can get this trip over and done with, the better.

Suddenly I almost wish we'd decided to head back over to Europe.

CHAPTER TWO

Nikki

"Why don't you take it easy and treat yourself tonight? You know, go out and do something. Hang out with one of your friends. I'm surprised you don't have a date lined up already." I know Mr. Harvey is just being polite, but I've always hated that comment, even coming from him. I smile.

"I mean, I've never really been one for relationships. And I don't know if going out is a good idea tonight. I mean, maybe it would be better if I stayed late and saw how Mr. Bridges gets on." I look over my shoulder, down the hall, but Mr. Harvey rests his hand on my arm, looking at me with compassion in his eyes. He sighs.

"Look, Nikki, I know it's not easy for you, but you've got to trust me on this. This isn't the kind of job where you can afford to take on everyone's problems. Your job is to sit there, listen, and offer advice, then go home and enjoy your evening at the end of the day." He tries to smile, but I shake my head, ignoring him.

Mr. Harvey has been a good friend, a mentor, and my boss since I came to work at Hope Hospital and Psychiatric Center, and I know he's right. He's been walking these halls for longer than I've been alive. Not only does he have the credentials, he's also got the experience to back up what he's saying, and no amount of arguing is going to change that.

But I can't help it.

Ever since I was a young girl, I've had a heart for others. It's part of the reason I went into therapy, and it's part of the reason I chose to work at this particular clinic. This clinic specializes in patients with severe anxiety and depression. This is the place people who struggle with substance abuse end up. This is the place where I can truly reach out and help those who are in need.

And lately, I've taken a particular liking to Mr. Bridges.

If I'm being honest, there's more than one reason for this. Not only is he a kind old man who is very lonely, but he's also the father of five boys I have always had crushes on.

Well, at one time they were boys. Now they are grown men, each with a solid rock and roll career. They formed the band in high school and, though not many in our peer group thought they'd make it very far, they are now selling out stadiums around the world and have an album on the verge of going platinum.

At least, that's what I've heard.

"Well, if you aren't going to make the decision for yourself, I'll make it for you. You've put in enough hours today, Nik. Go home, and I'll see you in the morning." Mr. Harvey brings my attention back to the present and I give him a grim smile.

I want to stay later and talk to Mr. Bridges some more. Even though he's not officially my patient, what with the conflict of interest and all, I still like to check in on him every day if I can. Today I want to hear him chat about his boys and how he hopes they're going to come visit him.

I don't want to go home to my lonely apartment.

But Mr. Harvey is my boss, and I have no choice. When he tells me to do something, I have to do it or I risk the possibility of being written up. I'm sure he wouldn't do that to me, knowing that it wouldn't look good on my résumé so shortly out of college.

But then, I don't want to tempt him. He doesn't wait for me to respond, turning and walking back up the hall toward the back rooms. Watching him walk away, I reach up and unbutton the top of my uniform as I try to decide what to do with my evening. If I have to go home, I may as well stop by the store and get something to treat myself with.

It's a Friday, after all, and if I'm going to be spending it alone on the couch with my Netflix account, I'm going to be doing it with a pint of ice cream.

"AND FINALLY, last but certainly not least, Lack of a Lover is going to be playing in town next week!" the voice on the radio cheerfully announces.

I look down at my dashboard in disbelief. Lack of a Lover is the Bridges boys' band. I know the clinic was going to try to get a hold of the brothers and let them know their father wanted to see them, but I haven't heard any updates, and I can't help but wonder now if they were successful.

"You don't say? They're our own boys! That's going to be a show to remember!" the other voice on the broadcast replies.

I roll my eyes. Small-town radio DJs are never very good at reporting any kind of local news, and these two young guys—

who I used to know in high school—are certainly living up to that standard.

I turn off my car, save for the lights and radio, in the parking lot of the grocery store. I want to go inside and get my ice cream so I can be out of there before the rest of the after-work crowds show up, but I have to hear the rest of this first. It's been years since I've thought of any of the Bridges, yet this week alone I've reconnected with their father and talked more about each of them than I ever thought I would again.

I blush as I think of the crushes I used to have on each of them. That family was certainly blessed in the gene department, and each of those boys had his own unique charm. At times, I would even be harboring a crush on more than one of them at the same time, making it even harder when they were both in the same room.

But I was awkward and homely in high school—certainly not the kind of girl any of the older brothers would have bothered giving a second glance.

Yes, I'm still a little bitter about that fact, but then there's another part of me that argues that it would be nice to see them again, despite the tinge of awkwardness I might feel at seeing my puberty-fueled, unrequited crushes again.

Perhaps they'll take the time to stop in and visit their father while they're in town. That will make his life far more bearable than it currently is, and the thought of it makes my heart skip a beat.

"Tickets are on sale now on our website, or you can plan on stopping in here at the studio to pick some up. I wouldn't wait—these are going to go fast!" the first voice chimes through the radio once more.

"It's about fucking time," I mutter as I grab my phone, relieved that they've finally given the information I was waiting to hear. I've made my decision, and I'm buying a ticket to the show. They've probably only improved with age. After all, I can't imagine they would be able to travel the world if they haven't.

I smile as I slip my phone in my purse. Suddenly, my night doesn't seem as dreary as it did. The concert's just a few days away, plenty close enough for me to start getting excited for it now.

In fact, I almost start thinking of this ice cream that I'm going to call dinner as something of a celebration.

Almost.

CHAPTER THREE

James

"I don't know, maybe if you'd changed your fucking number this wouldn't have happened? You know I don't want to have anything to do with him, and neither does anyone else!" I shake my head angrily, amazed that Tommy had the audacity to present such an idea.

"Look, James, I know you're upset. I was, too, at first. But this is Dad we're talking about. He might not have a lot of time left, and I would hate to think of how we would feel if we had this chance to go see him and didn't take it." Tommy gives me a look, the one he'd so often given us as kids, when he'd have to act like the dad our father never was.

"At the very least, it's only fair to tell everyone the message I got. We're going to be in the area anyway; if they want to see him, they can. If they don't, that's up to them." Tommy looks away as he continues to speak, and I shake my head. I know he's right. I would be fucking pissed if he'd gotten this message and hadn't told me. Perhaps even more pissed than I am right now.

"You realize the only reason we're going to be in the area anyway is because you and fucking Joe have decided to tour through the US. Last I heard we were going to be doing another European circuit." I cross my arms and give him a look. He might plan most of the trips with Joe, but I'm still aware of what's going on—more than he thinks I am.

"Again, this might be our only chance. I don't know how bad off Dad is. The chick who called me didn't say anything about how much time he had left, just that the cancer is spreading and she feels we should visit sooner rather than later." Tommy lights a cigarette, and I can sense he's growing agitated with the conversation. I don't give a fuck. I'm already agitated, and he can be, too, for all I fucking care.

"James, I know you're pissed off at what Dad did to us. We all are. But I also know you don't blame him entirely. We had a fucked-up childhood, but so did a ton of other kids. We can put it behind us to see him one more time, can't we? Besides, don't you want to shove it down everyone's throats how well we've been doing?" He grins and I can't help but smirk.

It's true. We certainly got our fair share of being picked on in high school. Not just through high school, but in junior high and as far back as we can remember. It's part of the reason I'm so angry with my father now. I remember going to him, time and time again, telling him that the kids at school were mean to us.

His answer was always the same.

If you want to make it in the real world, you'd better grow a pair and tell the bullies to fuck off.

It was good enough advice in and of itself, but none of us ever saw our father grow a pair himself. In fact, we all have vivid memories of him getting blackout drunk on a Tuesday night just because he had the bottle of whiskey in the fridge.

After our mom died when we were very young, he turned to alcohol to solve all his problems, and he was never able to give it up. It was a problem that only gained traction through the years, and by the time he was diagnosed with liver cancer, none of my brothers had much contact with him at all.

Sure, he liked to reason that our ungrateful attitudes were the reason we wanted nothing to do with him, but the fact of the matter is that it has less to do with us than it does with him. It has everything to do with the fact that he wasn't there for any of us when we needed him.

It certainly doesn't do a lot for me wanting to be there for him now. But then, I can't ignore the fact that Tommy had been like a second father to me—to all of us—and he has a real point. He doesn't want to see Dad anymore than any of us, but he also doesn't want us to end up living the rest of our lives filled with regret that we didn't let this go when we could have.

It's a fucked-up situation, and while I want it to just go away, I know for a fact it's not going to.

Besides, I have a sneaking suspicion Tanner is going to be all for going home. Bumfuck, Ohio—or Clayton, Ohio, as many prefer to call it—isn't just our hometown. It's Tanner's daughter's hometown too.

Now, none of us would ever call his daughter a mistake. Little Arya is by far one of the best things that has happened to any one of us, uncles or not. But it is safe to say that the little girl certainly wasn't planned, and though Tanner maintains next to no contact with the girl's mother, he's going to leap at the opportunity to see Arya again.

And I can't blame him for that. He doesn't have shared custody and is only limited to visitations. I guess it's to be expected, considering the life we so proudly lead. Though I can't help but wonder from time to time if he would change his lifestyle for a life with his daughter. Having no children of my own, I can't imagine that I can relate to how he feels about the situation, though I can speculate.

"When are you going to tell the others?" I ask, trying to embrace the more practical side of this situation. Tommy is nearly finished with his cigarette, and he takes another long drag before answering me.

"I already texted everyone. You're the only one who has bothered to respond." His words hang in the air for a few awkward moments, and I can't help but wonder how the rest of my brothers are taking the news. I can imagine they're all pissed off about it in one way or another, and I think it's perfectly understandable if none of them knows what to say.

This has come out of the blue for all of us, and I doubt I'm the only one who's going to need convincing that it's a good idea to go. Sure, Tanner might have the added incentive of seeing his daughter, but that doesn't mean Nathan or Janus will be on board.

As far as I know, Janus has made it clear that the next time he intends to see our father is when we're standing around his grave at his funeral. But then, if Tommy has been able to get through to me and convince me that this is a good idea, I'm sure he can get through to our younger brother as well.

"I'm sure they'll answer when they're fucked up enough to comprehend this," Tommy says after the moment of silence began to turn awkward. I nod. I could go for a cigarette myself right about now, but there are more pressing things that I need to tend to.

"I'm sure Joe's going to be in touch with the details, as he always is. He wants us down there within the next few days," Tommy calls after me.

I lift my hand to show him that I've heard, but I don't stop or turn around. It's the same old routine with Joe, and I know the drill. I don't need my brother to tell me how we're going to work this out.

We always do things the same way. Of course, I know he's just trying to fill the awkward void he's probably feeling himself right now by trying to micromanage. And I can't blame him for it.

I thought we were done with this hit—our hometown, our father. Now, evidently, we are not. So I better get used to the fact that some old, unpleasant memories and feelings might start to rear their ugly head.

In a matter of a few days, we will all be heading home.

CHAPTER FOUR

Tanner

"So what's your opinion? You think this is just something Dad's springing on us because he wants something, or do you think shit's finally catching up with him?" Janus looks from one face to the next, waiting for one of us to answer the question. Nobody answers.

How the fuck would any of us know what's going on inside Dad's head? And even if we did, will it ultimately change what we're going to do? This has got to be one of the most fucked-up decisions I've ever had to make, and if it weren't for my daughter, I don't think I would even consider going back home.

To be honest, even with my daughter there I'm not certain I want to go. I know how much it can fuck a kid up not to have a dad in their life, but at the same time, I know how much it can fuck a kid up to have a shitty dad in their life. I was that kid. I had a dad, sure, but he was one of the most fucked-up dads I can imagine.

There have been more times in my life when I wished he wasn't there than when I was glad that he was, and I don't ever want to make my daughter feel that way. I want to be a happy presence in her life, and if I'm going to do that, I have to get my shit together before I can make her a constant part in my life.

"The decision's all but been made. Joe's working out the hotel and everything right now. He's going to get back to me once he has more information," Tommy informs everyone. Janus still seems really pissed by the situation, but I can't think of a thing to say.

"At least you're going to get to see your kid," Nathan chimes in. It's the first he's spoken since Tommy told us of this fucked up situation, and I want nothing more than to tell him to fuck off. "That is, if you're going to bother to see her."

"I don't recall seeing you too excited about this whole thing, either," I snap back at him. I'm not going to take any shit from any of them. I don't care if they do have a point.

"And why the hell would I be excited about this? I was thinking we'd be heading back over to Germany, not the middle of nowhere, Ohio!" Nathan shoots back. He crosses his arms and I puff out my chest. I'm not afraid to get into a scuffle with any of my brothers. I might not be as big as they are, but they've never intimidated me.

"Calm the fuck down, both of you. The last thing we need is for one of us to show up with a black eye." James steps in between us, putting his hands on our chests and pushing us in opposite directions of the bar.

"James is right. Not to mention we don't need to make headlines before we head home. You know it's going to be bad enough being around ... everyone." Tommy drains the rest of his whiskey Coke and silence takes over among us for a few minutes.

He's right. There really isn't anyone back home that any of us want to see.

Besides Arya.

"Look, it's going to be two days, tops, and then we'll be moving on to the next town. Let's just fucking suck it up and pretend that it's another stop on the road. We can deal with the fans and Dad, and move on like it never happened. You know Dad doesn't have that much time left. I can't imagine this is going to take more than a couple days. It's not like it's going to change our lives." James looks from me to Janus and back again, and I sit down at my seat back at the table.

I don't say anything for a few minutes, listening to them bicker about the set we're going to play and what we're going to do in the off time we've got. If there's any luck, we aren't going to have a lot of off time, and any that we have, I'll be spending with my daughter.

Just my daughter. Not with Caitlyn.

I shudder at the thought. I have only spoken to Caitlyn a few times in the past couple months, and it was about Arya each time. The pure and simple fact of the matter is that I don't like talking to her, and I don't want to do so anymore than I absolutely have to.

There was a time when I thought Caitlyn was the woman I would marry. She was perfect in every sense of the word, and I was thrilled when we were together. There wasn't a single thing about her I would've changed, and I know she felt the same about me.

But stress can put a major damper on a relationship. I was trying to get the band launched. I was having a tough time dealing with the stress caused by the strained relationship with my dad, and to make matters worse, my brothers all assumed that because I had the best relationship with him out of all of us, that I was the one who would know what was going on.

But I didn't know anything more than anyone else did.

I know I didn't handle things well with Caitlyn, but when the chance came, I left. I packed up my things and headed out with the rest of the band, ready to take on a new life. Ready to forget the past. I knew it would break her heart, and I felt like a piece of shit for doing it, but I reminded myself that I would get over it, and so would she.

I figured that, with time, we'd each forget about the other, or when we did think about each other, we'd think about how foolish we were in high school and leave it at that.

At least, that is what I convinced myself would happen. When I finally heard from her nearly a year later, she let me know that she had a daughter. No, she let me know that *we* had a daughter.

Needless to say, I was blindsided and was completely livid, demanding we have a test done to prove that I was the child's biological father. Any hopes of having an amicable breakup with Caitlyn went out the window at that point. When the test came back positive and I knew for certain she was mine, I thought my life was over.

That is, until I met the little girl.

From the moment I laid my eyes on her, I knew I loved her more than anything. At that moment, it no longer mattered who her mother was. All that mattered was that this precious little angel was half me, and I was going to do everything in my power not to fuck up her life the same way my father fucked up mine.

I would give her the world—but I knew that that might be best accomplished if I stayed out of hers.

"You okay, buddy?" Tommy asks as he takes a seat next to me, and I suddenly realize the others have gone off to shoot a game of pool. I finish the drink in front of me and nod.

"Yeah, fan-fucking-tastic," I say, my voice strained. He slaps me on the shoulder and gives me a light shake, giving me the same smile he always has over the years. If there's anyone in my group of brothers I expect to kind of understand what I'm feeling, it's Tommy.

We might be at each other's throats a lot, but I know he cares about the shit I'm doing.

"You know you'll be glad to see her as soon as you do," he says with a grin. I nod and he slaps my shoulder once more before getting up and heading into the lobby to shoot pool with the rest. I hesitate. I want to argue, but I know he's right.

I might tell myself that I don't want to get involved in her life because I don't want to fuck her up, but the fact is I'll do anything to see my daughter again, even if it's only for a few minutes. I just want to take her in my arms and tell her how beautiful she is; I want to stroke her hair and tell her to her face that I love her more than anything else in this world.

Yes, I'll do anything to make that happen.

Even if it means I'll have to visit my fucking father.

CHAPTER FIVE

ikki

"Did you hear? They're coming home! My boys are coming home!" Mr. Bridges sounds elated as he sits up in his chair, looking at me with brimming eyes. I smile and look down at my notes. I'm not supposed to get overly emotional in front of patients, and I am determined to set up some boundaries.

At the same time, I feel his anticipation. He hasn't seen any of his sons in over five years, and I can't imagine what he must be feeling. He's told me more than once the regret he feels over how they were raised, and the things he wishes he could go back and do over.

I try to tell him that mistakes are in the past, and that he has to focus on what he can do now. I pray he hears me, but I'm not so certain he does.

"I'm sure they're all going to be very excited to see you. I heard they're also putting on a show while they're here," I say, trying to move the subject along. I know he can get stuck talking about this for the rest of the day if I let him, and that's not what I want to do.

"I heard that as well, but I can't say I'm going to make it. I'm hoping they'll be happy with coming here to see me, or I can go somewhere quiet where we could talk." Mr. Bridges looks out the window, and I can see he's wracking his brain for any idea of how he can get together with his sons.

I almost offer a solution, but I remember what Mr. Harvey told me.

"Your job is to listen, first and foremost. You can offer advice if they ask for it, but don't shove your solutions on everyone as soon as they pose a problem. Our goal is to give these people purpose and rational solutions for their issues, not solve their problems for them."

Mr. Bridges might not be my official patient, but I know I should still follow the rules.

"I don't know. This damned cancer isn't letting me get far from bed, so I'm thinking our best bet is if they come here. What do you say? Would you mind setting that up for me? I would be eternally grateful to you if you did." Mr. Bridges suddenly turns his attention back to me, reaching out and taking both my hands in his.

I hesitate. I've been wondering myself if I want to go through with a face-to-face meeting with any of the men. There was a time when we were decently good friends, but I've always felt a little hurt at the way they ditched me when they all left. It was like I was part of the nightmare they wanted to get away from, and they hardly bothered saying goodbye.

In a way, we almost grew up together. They lived a few blocks up from me and I was the grade beneath Tanner in school. In fact, there was a time when Tanner and I were an item, dating for a few months my freshman year. Sure, nothing came of it and he moved on to another girl before they left, and I have to admit that I did have a crush on his brothers from time to time as well, but it was still ... *something*.

I always knew who their father was, but it wasn't until I went to school and became a therapist that I started to understand a bit more about what they were dealing with. I knew he was an angry man who was almost always drunk, but I didn't know the extent of the problems that were happening in the family.

I can't blame them for not speaking to their father now that they are old enough to be on their own. But I can blame them for disappearing from my life as they did.

They were there one day, then they were gone the next.

"Please? You know I don't have any way to really get a hold of them, and I'm afraid if I don't stay on them, they won't come. This could be my last chance to see any of them. God knows what this cancer is doing to me!" He looks down at his body, and I feel sorry for him. There is the nudge in the back of my mind, telling me not to get overly involved in the situation, but I can't turn down this dying man's request.

Not to mention the fact that the more I've gotten to know this man, the more compassion I've felt for him. My own strained relationship with my father makes me crave male attention of any kind, but it is rare for anyone to treat me as though I am their daughter.

In fact, I went into psychology and therapy because I wanted to make my father proud. If it had been left up to me, I would have done exactly what the Bridges boys did. I would have gone into performing arts of some kind.

But my father thought it all rather ridiculous and made it clear that if I was to do anything of value with my life, I had better get into something that paid the bills. He basically forced me into the medical field.

But I went through with it, and now that I am in a position to help this man, I know it's what I have to do.

He very specifically asked me for help, and I know his days are limited. I close my notebook and set it on my lap, bringing my legs together and looking at him with a bright smile.

"You know what? I bet we can do that very thing. It might not be easy to get them all down here at the same time, or for very long if they have a show scheduled, but I can promise you I'll do everything in my power to make sure they come in and see you before they leave." I feel my heart sinking as I speak, my confidence leaving me as I finish my speech. I don't know if I'm making this man a promise I can't keep, but I've said it with such conviction that there's little doubt in my mind he believes what I'm saying.

He reaches forward once more and puts his hands over mine, gently squeezing them in his palms and giving me a broad smile.

"I knew I could count on you. If there's anyone in the world who can make this happen for me, it's you!" He laughs and looks out the window once more, and I start to feel very nervous. I would think that I am the last one anyone would ask to try to pull off such a thing.

It's no secret to the town that the boys and their father have never gotten along. Since becoming the man's confidante I've gotten more inside information that leaves me unable to blame them for writing him off once they were on their own.

But I've always been a compassionate person, and I can't say no to his request. I can see in his eyes how desperately he wants to make things right with his sons, and I'm not going to let a little difficulty stand in the way of me at least trying to make that happen.

"I am going to do everything in my power to get them here as soon as I can," I say with a warm smile. I rise from my seat and look at the bed.

"Do you need assistance getting back in there?" I ask. He

looks over his shoulder at the bed as well, then shakes his head and gives me a dismissive wave of his hand.

"I can manage. There are a few things I would like to do for myself, as long as I can. Thank you so much for your kind words, and let me know the moment you hear from them!" He smiles and gets out of the chair slowly, and I fight the urge to hurry over and help him.

I want to make sure he's as comfortable as I can possibly make him, and it worries me to see him struggle.

"Ring if you need anything," I say as I walk toward the door. He's settling into the pillows, looking happier than I have seen him in months. I smile to myself as I close the door most of the way behind me. I don't want to think of what Mr. Harvey will say about my promise. I don't want to think of the reality of how hard it's going to be to pull off.

Right now, I just want to go into my next appointment knowing that, at least for now, I have made that man happier than he has been in years. It's not going to be easy. In fact, it might be impossible for to get a hold of any of his sons, but I'm sure as hell going to try my best.

After all, there was a time when they were my friends. They should make the time to see me. Famous or not, we were friends.

I deserve at least a little of their attention.

CHAPTER SIX

Tommy

"And you all thought we weren't going to make it!" Greg, our bus driver, looks over his shoulder with a grin, but I ignore him.

He's right—I didn't think we were going to make it, and I'm still surprised we did. I want to tell him to fuck off, but I'll be nice. He did get us down here, though I'm still pissed at Joe for not getting us plane tickets like I suggested.

"I'm no mechanic, but I think we should get the bus to a garage as soon as possible," Janus says as he steps toward the front. I adjust the paper on my lap, still refusing to say anything. I get so fucking tired of these guys never listening to me. I'll let them figure this one out.

Tanner follows Janus toward the front of the bus, but he's scanning the parking lot we've pulled into. I don't blame him. He's been staring out the window since we got to town, and I know he's hoping for even just a glimpse of his daughter. It's unlikely we'll see her now, since it's school hours, but I know he's thinking about her more than he's willing to admit.

"Well, what do you want to do, Tommy? I can take you guys over to the hotel and let you get settled in. You can check in with Joe and see what he wants to do with the bus, but with the smoke billowing out of the engine," at this, he points out the window to a small cloud of smoke that's hovering ominously around the front of the bus, "we aren't going to be getting very far." Greg turns his attention to me, and I roll my eyes.

"You're the driver. I think that of anyone here, you'll be able to figure this out, Greg. Anyway, I don't want to get stranded in the middle of the road, here of all places. Let's call an Uber and get the fuck out of here. You can figure this shit out and give me a call when you've got an update." I ignore the look he gives me and grab my phone, ordering an Uber.

I don't give a fuck how long it takes him to get to the mechanic. I'd much rather be settled into the hotel room right now with a cold beer in my hand. We've just spent hours on the road, and I refuse to let myself think about it too much or I'll get pissed off at Joe all over again.

By the time we get to the hotel, all of us are hot and hungry, but I'm in better spirits than I was. There's something about being back home that brings back a lot of memories, even the ones that I thought I didn't want to remember. As the oldest in the family, I am the one who lived here the longest, and I remember the trouble James and I used to get into after school.

"Look, Tommy. Isn't that the old dumpster we threw Hansen in during junior year?" James calls up from the back seat. I look out the window at the old parking lot with the large graffitied dumpster and laugh, looking back at him. We hated that kid, and it felt good throwing him into the dumpster.

Sure, it might've been considered bullying, but the little shit wouldn't leave Tanner alone. We weren't going to stand by and watch some entitled asshole pick on our little brother.

We get to the hotel and I'm relieved to hear Joe has everything set up. It only takes a few minutes to get us each settled in our private rooms. Another thing I'm glad he had the brains to arrange.

My phone rings.

"What?" I ask, putting it up to my ear.

"Well, I've got some good news and some bad news." Joe's voice comes through the phone. I'm surprised it isn't Greg, and I check the number to make sure it's right.

"What news?" I ask impatiently.

"Greg called and said you guys were having issues with the bus on the way down there," Joe continues. I agree, still letting the annoyance shine through in my voice.

"Well, it turns out we're going to need to do something with the engine before you're able to move on with the tour. I have the part on the way already, but they're looking at the end of the week before they're going to be able to put it in." Joe is speaking in his matter-of-fact tone. The one he uses when he knows he's giving me shit I don't want to hear.

"And what the fuck does that mean for the tour?" I ask. I don't want to hang out in this town any longer than we have to, but I can sense that's where this conversation is going.

"Settle down, Tommy. That's where the good news comes in." I relax, thinking he's going to get us out of here on time.

He isn't.

"It turns out both the shows have already sold out. So we decided to go ahead and extend it for two more nights. That's going to push you pretty close to the end of the week, and I can fly all of you out of there and on to the next show. The bus can follow, and we'll be back on track by the beginning of next week if all goes according to plan." He sounds optimistic, but I'm not sharing his enthusiasm.

"You know as well as I do that things rarely go according to plan," I snap.

"There's not much we can do about this right now. Unless you all want to cough up the hundreds of dollars it'll take for you to make it to the next show—with all your gear—in an Uber, you're stuck there, my friend. Come on, it's not so bad. I thought you wanted to see your dad and shit?" Joe tries to change the subject, and I cringe.

I am willing to see our father, but he's not the main reason we're here. Or is he? I can't even remember, with all the news that's been thrown at me over the past couple of days, and with all the emotions I'm feeling being home again.

"Yeah, we're going to fit in seeing him at some point, but my main focus at the moment is to get out of here. I have a job to do, Joe. We all do." I change the subject back to work. I would rather talk about work with my agent than my personal life, and I smile to myself as I hear him sigh. At least I'm not the only one having to deal with the stress of all this.

"I know, I know, and I'm doing the best I can. Look, I'm going to get on the phone with the airline as soon as I'm done with you, and I'll see what I can work out. You, on the other hand, focus on catching up with some old friends. Work on the shows. It's been years since you've played your hometown, and you did say you wanted to put on a show no one is going to forget." Joe once again sounds optimistic, and I sigh.

I know he's right. There are a lot of people in this town I would like to prove a point to. But even that all comes back to my father. He's the one, above all else, that I want to prove to that I've done something with my life. I'm not sure how I'm going to do that, though.

I can't see him coming to any of the shows. Not in the condition he's in. No. If I want to show him what I've accomplished, I'm going to have to do it face to face.

I wrap up the conversation with Joe and hang up my phone, taking another sip of my beer.

There is no doubt in my mind that whenever I speak to my father again, it's going to be a conversation neither of us will soon to forget.

CHAPTER SEVEN

James

"Okay, okay, that's about all I've got in me. Thank you, thank you. Tell your friends and don't miss the show tomorrow night!" I smile, but it fades as I duck into the dive bar. I'm starving. I've spent all day taking photos with fans and giving out autographs, and I'm ready for something to eat.

I have to admit, I was surprised by the turnout at the show last night. For being such a small town, we certainly tore up the stage and had a good time. When Joe said that we sold out the stadium, I didn't know he meant the largest venue in town.

It felt good. There were many faces in the crowd I recognized. Many of which I remembered taunting me back in the day, telling me I wasn't going to make it—not in music, and not in life. Well, who are they all fighting to get an autograph from now?

"James?" A somewhat familiar voice calls me, and I turn around, looking confused. I know that most of the people in town know who I am, but there is something about the voice that is all too familiar. I know it belongs to someone I used to know quite well, but I just can't place it.

I turn around, and to my utter shock, Nikki Marlow is standing in front of me. My heart skips a beat and I feel my tongue catch in the back of my throat. I haven't seen, or even thought, of the girl since just after high school. Now here she is in front of me, looking as gorgeous as I remember her, though much more mature.

She has to be close to her mid-twenties by now. I have no idea what she's been up to since we left town, but she looks like she could be a model. Petite, slender, with an athletic frame that immediately sends my mind into the gutter. Her bright green eyes are looking at me with a sparkle I remember well, and her brunette hair is pulled back into a tight ponytail.

"James Bridges, it's been forever!" she continues. I still can't find the words as she takes a step forward and pulls me into a hug. Finally, I feel my tongue release and I smile, pulling her back and looking down at her.

"Nikki Marlow! My God, look at you! You've grown up!" I suddenly feel old, not knowing what else to say, and she gives me a playful look.

"I guess you could say that. I went to your show last night, you know. I had a blast." She winks, and I feel pride swell up in my chest. She was always one of the more encouraging people in our lives, but it's still good to hear that she enjoyed the show.

"I didn't see you, but you can't hold it against me—that was a big crowd," I joke. I'm still scrambling for what to say to her, but I know I don't want the conversation to end.

"Yeah." She continues to smile at me with her sparkling eyes. "Anyway," she goes on, "I'm working as a therapist now and, small world, your father is one of the patients at my clinic! He knows you're in town and was wondering if there might be a way for you to stop by and visit him. I told him I would do my best to set it up." She's still smiling, but there's a tension in her face now and I can sense she doesn't know how I'm going to react.

I put my hand on the back of my neck and look away.

"Yeah, the clinic got a hold of Tommy and he told us Dad wasn't doing so well. We were planning on stopping in to see him at some point, but I'm not the one who's usually in charge of these things." I smile, but I can see by the look in her eyes that she doesn't fully believe me.

She returns my look and waves her hand with a light shake of her head. "That's totally understandable, and I can imagine you guys are really busy. Like I said, I told him I'd do my best. I think he'll understand if you have too much going on."

I can tell by the look in her eyes that she's merely trying to keep the peace, but I'm still relieved when she changes the subject. "So anyway, how is everyone? I haven't spoken to any of you since ... gosh, it's been years!"

"I know! We've been living a pretty crazy life lately—lots of traveling and shows and all that shit. You wouldn't believe how much work goes into putting out a song," I joke with her once more, trying to keep the conversation on anything other than my father.

"I can imagine. I always wanted to go into music or something, but my dad wanted me to get into the medical field. He said it would pay the bills better, but I guess he never followed your career." She laughs and I join in. I don't remember her father well, but I do remember him being overbearing. I never cared for him much.

"Well, I'm sure he's proud of what you do," I reply. There is a brief silence before she looks around.

"Anyway, I just thought I would come say hey since it's been so long. I'm glad to hear that you're doing well, and if you decide you're going to come in and see your dad, I'll see you then!" She gives me another cheerful, light hug, but I sense there's more she wants to say.

"Most definitely. I'd love to see you around again before we head out," I say. There's another awkward silence, more charged this time, then she gives me a light nod and leaves. I hesitate, trying to process what just happened.

Watching her, I see her pause suddenly and come back. There's a look on her face that tells me she's either nervous or has just remembered something she wants to tell me. Or perhaps it's a mix of both.

"Here, let me give you my personal number. It's a much faster way to get a hold of me, rather than trying to get through the clinic. And feel free to give it to any of your brothers if they want to set up a time to come see him." She jots down her number on the corner of a napkin and hands it to me before once more smiling and turning to go.

I sit there for another moment, still a bit bemused by the interaction.

I can't believe, between the five of us, that not one of us thought about Nikki Marlow when we talked about coming back here. Or, at least, I didn't. I don't know if anyone else did, but if they did, they certainly didn't say anything about it. I grab my phone from my pocket and quickly dial Tommy.

"Hello?" His voice comes through the phone.

"Dude, do you have a sec?" I ask.

"Yeah, what's up?" he replies.

"You'll never guess who I just ran into!"

CHAPTER EIGHT

Tanner

"Look, Caitlyn, we've already agreed that we don't have to be friends. We don't even have to fucking like each other. All I want is to get to see my daughter!" I'm trying to keep my cool, but I'm feeling an explosive mix of emotions.

Caitlyn Thomas, my daughter's mother, is being extremely difficult. And hearing her voice again—knowing we're in the same town—is more than I want to deal with right now. I know it's not fair of me to have walked out on her the way I did, then to come back into town without giving her any kind of warning, but hell, that's the life of a rock star.

"I have therapy sessions and she has school. Maybe if you had told me before you were in town then I would have had the time to set up something! You can't just show up and expect everyone to cater to you because you've chosen to grace us with your presence," she snaps through the phone.

I can understand her position, but I'm too angry to be reasonable with her. From my point of view, I can't understand why she doesn't drop some of the less important shit if it means her daughter will get to see her father. There is no doubt in my mind that Arya will love to see me as much as I will love to see her.

Besides, I prefer it if Caitlyn isn't there for the meeting, anyways. But, if she feels more comfortable supervising, I honestly don't give a fuck about it one way or the other.

"I get that, and I apologize. But you have to realize I had no idea we were going to be coming through town right now. Last I heard we were going to be heading back through Europe, but I guess there's shit going down with my dad so they moved some dates around." I let my voice trail off, but she catches it.

"So you can come through for the father you hate but you can't take the time to come through to see your daughter? How do you think that makes her feel? Do you have any idea how hard it is for me to tell her why you aren't a part of her life? I don't like seeing her upset, Tanner. I can get over what you did to me, but I am not going to ask her to get over what you did to her." She's speaking too quickly for me to interject, and I sit calmly, allowing her to finish her rant before I speak again.

"Caitlyn, you know we didn't plan on living this life, but now that we are, we have to make the most of it. I'm not asking you to not hate me. I'm not asking you to do anything, really. All I want is the chance to see my daughter while I'm in town. If I can find a way to extend my stay so I can see her when it works better for you, I will be happy to do that, but that's really all I can do." I don't like pleading with her. I don't like pleading with anyone.

I hate this feeling of being vulnerable. Even more than that, I hate knowing that someone else has this kind of power over me. I know Caitlyn can prevent me from seeing Arya at all while I'm here, and she knows it, too. I know that I treated her badly—that

I treated both of them badly—years before, and I know I can't expect her to just forget about all of it now. But still, it sucks.

There are a few moments of silence before I hear her sigh through the phone.

"Maybe if you can find a way to extend your trip for a few days I can find the time to get her to you. But I'm not going to disrupt her school schedule or any of the other things she has planned, and you have to understand that it's just as important for her that I go to therapy as it is for me." Her voice is hot and testy, and I know she's just itching for a fight.

Caitlyn has always made therapy a huge priority in her life. Any time anything has ever gone wrong in her life, she has turned to medication and a therapist. I used to fight with her about it when we were dating—that she used to rely on it too much, that it was becoming just as much of a crutch as any other bad habit—but it was something that I eventually learned to let slide.

I always figured if I was able to get through my life without it, she should be able to as well. Caitlyn, on the other hand, argued that if I were to go to therapy myself then I would be much happier and would be able to deal with a lot of the shit from my past that still bothers me.

As it stands, and as it will likely always stand between us, we aren't going to see the other person's point of view, nor will either of us be willing to change our own points of view. In our minds, one of us has to be right and the other wrong.

"All right, that's all I'm asking. I'm going to talk to the rest of the band and make sure they can find someone to cover for me, and I'll get back to you as soon as I can. Just remember that you're doing this for Arya, not for me." I hope if the focus stays on our daughter she'll be less likely to change her mind before I have the chance to see them.

"Keep me in the loop this time. If you aren't going to be able to see her, just let me know, okay? You've shown in the past that you're willing to just drop people as soon as they become inconvenient to you, and if you ever try to do that to Arya, you can rest assured that you are never going to see her again. Do you understand?"

I feel the tension rising in my chest. I want to argue with her, tell her to fuck off and quit acting like I'm a terrible father just because I was a terrible boyfriend.

At the same time, I know she has a point. I can't do that to my daughter. It will destroy her. If I am going to make plans to see her, then it doesn't matter what the rest of the band does. Even if it means we have to miss a show, I have to be there for my daughter.

It would just be so much fucking easier if Caitlyn would bend and let me see her now, without me having to change things around.

"I get it. I'll keep you in the loop," I say. We both hang up after a tense, brief goodbye, and I sigh as I throw the phone on my hotel bed.

I bury my face in my hands and rub my eyes, trying to rid myself of the headache that set in shortly after starting the conversation. I wish I could get control of the emotions that are running through my mind, and I know it's a result of the fact I'm going to have to see Caitlyn at some point.

I tell myself that I don't want to see her. I tell myself that I only want to see Arya. But the truth is, I'm dying to see them both. Even though we have trouble getting along now, the sound of her voice is enough to make my heart skip a beat, and I just want give her a hug.

Forgetting Caitlyn has never been as easy as I thought it would be when I left her.

I walk over to my mini fridge and pour myself a drink. If there's one thing that will get my mind off my ex, it's whiskey.

As I drain the glass and look at the empty mug in my hands, I briefly think about what it would be like to get back together with Caitlyn. We'd be an actual family, me and her and Arya.

I quickly shake my head, trying to get the thought out before it has the audacity to go any further. The very idea of such a thing ever happening is so ludicrous, I could laugh.

I'll get to see my daughter, and that will be the end of that. To take my mind off things, I decide to log onto one of my many social media accounts. There's always good shit going on online, and it'll relieve some of the stress I'm feeling about how and when I'm going to get to see my little girl.

After all, I'll just have to take what I can get.

CHAPTER NINE

Nikki

I sip on the glass of wine next to my laptop, trying to focus on the screen in front of me. I've been doing what I can to settle down and relax after work, hoping that I will sleep better if I do. My phone rings and I glance down, part of me hoping it's someone inviting me to come back in to work.

I cringe, realizing it's my dad. Reluctantly, I pick up the phone and put it to my ear.

"Hello?"

"You haven't called in a while. Thought I would check up on you and remind you that you still have a dad." My dad sounds agitated, and I prepare myself for the fight that's inevitably about to start.

"I'm sorry. I've been really swamped at work and busy trying to make things meet day to day, you know? I don't mean to let so much time pass between calls." I silently pray he'll let it go, but I can hear in his tone he's not going to.

"I should think if I were important to you, you'd make a bigger effort to talk to me."

"Look, Dad, I'm sorry. I've been busy—" I try, but he interrupts.

"I don't want to hear your excuses! Now, how are your finances? Are you making enough money with the new job?" I cringe once more. I've been at my job for a few months now. It's not exactly new anymore, but I know my dad has high hopes that I'm going to be bringing in a lot more money than I am.

"I'm doing all right. I've been doing what I can to make ends meet, and like I said, juggling my busy schedule can make it difficult to know how I'm doing exactly." I laugh, but I can hear by the sound of his breathing on the other end of the line that he's not nearly as amused as I am.

"Anyway, how are things going for you?" I quickly try to change the subject. "It's been a while since I've gotten to hear from you, and I was hoping you'd give me a call," I lie. I know my father is really calling to bitch about something, probably me, but it sounds better than letting him know that I treasure the periods of silence between us.

"Oh, you know. Trying to take care of myself since my only child doesn't seem to give a shit about me anymore." I know he's being manipulative, and I'm doing my best not to get drawn in.

"Daddy, you know that's not true. I just have my own life now, and I'm just trying to focus on getting everything done in a day that needs doing. I will always have the time for you when you need me!" I hope my fake enthusiasm is convincing, but I can hear by the next sigh that he's still not impressed.

"Daddy, I've really got to get going. You caught me at just the right time to say hello, but I've got to get working again shortly. You know how it goes." I cut him off when he tries to complain once more and hang up the phone as soon as I can. The last thing I want is to have it out with my dad right now. There are too many things running through my mind.

I look up at the ceiling, fighting the urge to pour myself a second glass of wine. The last thing I want is to get drunk on a night when I have to be at work early the next day. That sounds about as intelligent as trying to make things work with my father.

I turn my attention back to the screen in front of me, trying to get him out of my mind. I notice in the corner of the computer that Tanner is also logged on to Messenger. I hesitate, my heart pounding in my chest.

It's been years since I've spoken to him. So many times over the years I've noticed him logged in, and I've hidden his icon, removing the temptation to reach out to him. We didn't even date for that long, but he's always taken up space at the back of my mind. I like to believe that I'm over him, but the truth is that I don't feel like I ever got the closure with him that I really wanted.

Then, next thing I knew, he was a dad. Not to mention he left town without a backward glance and never came back. There seems to be no point in rehashing old feelings and old flames. But I can't shake the urge, so I send him a brief message.

Hey! Went to your show last night! Looking good!

My heart thuds in my chest as I see that he's read the message and then begins typing an answer.

Hey! It's been a while. Good to hear from you. James said he ran into you earlier. Crazy, right? How have you been?

My heart continues to pound in my chest as we continue trading messages. It feels so great to talk to him after all this time, but there's so much I want to tell him. Throughout the conversation, though, I sense that he's looking for an out, an end to our chat, or perhaps I'm just being paranoid.

At last, I ask him.

No, it's not you. I had a bit of an upsetting conversation with Caitlyn Thomas the other day. You remember her? She isn't making it easy to see my daughter, and that's really all I want to do.

I take a deep breath, feeling conflicted. I know that I can set that up for him, and there is a small part of me that wants to help. But at the same time, the mention of his ex and their daughter fills me with a weird sense of jealousy.

What if we never broke up? Would we have a child together now?

But then, another thought forms in the back of my mind. Perhaps if I help him see his daughter, it will put me in his good graces. Perhaps he'll even want to rekindle our old friendship. Before we dated, we were really good friends, and aside from whatever other confusing feelings I have toward him, I do miss that friendship.

After a brief moment of hesitation, I begin to type.

You know, Caitlyn is a patient at my clinic. I can't give you any details on her, and I probably shouldn't even be sharing this much, but if you want to see your daughter, she usually brings her with her when she comes to her appointments. I can give you a time, and you could "accidentally" be there when she is.

I hit send, my heart pounding. I know if he turns this in that I could lose my job, and I'm silently praying that he doesn't freak out at the unprofessionalism of my offer. My heart skips a beat as I see he's typing a reply.

Would you?

I smile as I sit back in my chair, relief washing over me. This isn't going to be easy, even with him cooperating with me. But I know that it's something we can pull off, and more than anything, I want to help him pull it off.

I wait a moment, then lean forward, hunched over my keyboard once more.

You know I will.

But we have to be careful. I could seriously get in trouble for this ...

We continue to chat for a couple of hours, our conversation turning from his daughter to what we've been up to for the past few years. As we talk, we easily slip back into the flirty banter we were so good at when we were teens. The more attention he gives me, the more I can feel those old feelings swelling up in the back of my mind. I know it's dangerous to dwell on them, but I can't get him out of my head.

As it starts to get late, I know I have to sign off and get some sleep, or there's no way I'm going to be up the next morning in time for my shift. I tell him so, and wait eagerly for the reply.

Sounds good. Get some rest, you goofball. Thank you again so much for doing this for me. I'll stop by and see Caitlyn as soon as I can.

I read the message and sign off, doing my best to smile to myself as I do. I know I should be proud of myself for setting up the meeting between him and his daughter, but I can't shake that weird tinge of jealousy, or regret, or whatever it is, that's in the back of my mind.

I don't want to think about him and Caitlyn together. I only want to focus on the fact he's going to get to see his daughter again. That's why I did this, so he can see his daughter again. He deserves that.

And thanks to me, he's going to get to see her much sooner than he thought.

CHAPTER TEN

Tommy

I sit with my phone to my ear, my heartrate slightly elevated. It's been years since I've spoken to Nikki Marlow, and I don't know exactly what I'm going to say to her. I remember her vaguely from when all the kids on the block used to hang out together. At least, I think it's a vague memory.

When James told me he ran into her, I felt another wave of emotions run through me. I always thought she was cute and that she and Tanner made a nice couple. In a way, once she got older, I always wanted to do something more with her. But when she and Tanner broke up toward the end of high school, I was more worried about what we were going to do with the band than anything.

Not to mention she was nearly seven years my junior. At the time she was with Tanner, she looked so young and innocent to me that I didn't think I could bring myself to do anything with her without feeling guilty about it. Simply feeling attracted to her made me feel like a dirty old man, even if I was only in my early twenties myself at the time.

Then, I forgot about her completely.

"Hello?" Her voice comes through the phone, distracting me from my thoughts. Sweet and familiar, like a breath of fresh air.

"Hey, this is Tommy Bridges. You might remember me?" I say quickly.

"Of course! Tommy! I went to your show the other night and thought it was great. Then I saw James at the diner downtown a couple days ago. You remember the one?" I do. I tell her that he gave me her number and she laughs.

"I figured that's how you got it. I don't give it out to many people, and I can't imagine most of the ones who do take it are too eager to hand it out."

"Do you get asked out that often, then?" I ask. The words are out of my mouth before I have the time to catch them, and she laughs once more.

"Oh, every now and then. I didn't stay the ugly duckling you said I was, you know." I cringe. I hoped she forgot about that, but it's clear she hasn't. I didn't mean it when I said it, but it's evident she thought that I did.

"I was teasing, you know. You were far from ugly. Anyway." I take a deep breath, hoping she'll leave it at that. "I wanted to set up a meeting with my father. But I don't want the media to get involved, if you know what I mean. Can we talk about this in person?" Again, I'm not sure why I let the words fly out of my mouth so quickly, and I'm surprised when she agrees.

"Let's meet at Greenie's Coffeehouse. I like it down there," she says.

We agree on a time and we hang up the phone. I sigh. I don't know if I should dress up, or if I'm fine in what I always wear. The debate is short-lived.

I'll go in what I always wear.

"Tommy! Over here!" She's motioning for me to meet her at the table, and my heart nearly stops. When James told me she'd gotten hot, I believed him—she was always cute—but I didn't expect this. I can hardly believe what I'm seeing.

She's much older than I remember her being. At least, she looks much older—and a thousand times hotter—than I remember. Her cheeks are flushed with excitement, and she pulls me in for a hug.

"It's good to see you! So good to see you!" she says as we take our seats. It takes me a moment before I'm able to find my tongue, but I finally find the words.

"It's good to see you as well. It really is," I assure her. I can't take my eyes off her body, though I am trying to force myself to look into her eyes. She laughs and I can see she's flattered by my unintentionally obvious attention, though she quickly turns the conversation to my father.

"I want to be clear that he doesn't want any drama. He's sorry for the way he was when you were growing up, and he's made it clear to me that he wants to make it right with you. He just doesn't know how." She's looking down into her cup of coffee as she speaks, and I have a difficult time keeping my eyes off her.

"That's what I want too. No drama, low-key. I don't know how many of my brothers are going to come with me for the initial meeting, or if there's going to be a point when more than one of us shows up at a time. But with that said, I don't want this shit on the news." I look at her searchingly, and I can see by the smirk on her face she's amused.

"Yes, I know what you mean. You've said that a couple of times now, and I want to assure you that you can relax. Of course

I won't do anything that's going to embarrass you or him. I don't want you to think that I ever would." She smiles once more, and I feel myself relax a bit.

I've been stressing about the logistics of getting us to meet with our dad, and I can't speak for my brothers, but I've hoping this will all be as easy as possible. If what she says is true, then it doesn't sound to me like meeting with him is going to very difficult at all.

Then again, just because setting up a meeting is easy, doesn't mean it's a good idea. Things like this always seem to be a good idea until I'm actually in them, and then I just want to find an exit as soon as possible.

"Well, that's a relief," I tell her truthfully. Looking at her sitting there with her pretty smile, it suddenly seems a shame that our meeting should end so quickly. "So, you're a therapist? How'd that come about? What have you been up to these last few years?"

Our conversation flows easily as we talk about her life and mine, and I can't believe how much she's matured. It's like she's an entirely new person from who she was, and I want to know her better.

"Hey, do you want to grab a drink with me tomorrow night? Just the two of us. I'd like the chance to get to talk to you when I'm not feeling so tense about the situation with my father," I say with a smile. I don't know what the fuck is wrong with me. For the first time in as long as I can remember, I feel nervous.

There's no reason I should be spending my time here, wining and dining a woman, when my schedule is already packed, but I want to be around her more. I can't place exactly why, besides the fact that she reminds me of home. She brings back good memories that I thought I wanted to forget, but I'm seeing now that I had a lot of good times in this town too. I don't want to forget everything about this little town.

In fact, there are parts of it I want to embrace one more time. It might be the last time I ever find myself here, but even if that's the case, I'm going to enjoy it.

She smiles as she turns back to me, and I can see clearly in her eyes that she feels flattered by my invitation. She has guileless eyes, like she's never told a lie in her life. It's refreshing.

"I'd love to," she says. A smile spreads across my own face and I give her a slight nod.

"Great. It's a date."

CHAPTER ELEVEN

James

"All I'm saying is that I would rather get it over with all together than have each of us trickling in and out of there. Don't you think Dad wants to see all of us at once? Then we don't have to worry about doing it again, and we can focus on getting the band out of here." Tommy's voice sounds irritated, but I'm only half listening.

He wants to get the meeting with Dad over with this afternoon. While I don't see any real reason why it won't work for us to meet with him, I don't want to be the one to break the news to my brothers. It's been clear to all of us that we are going to have to see the man eventually, but we've all been pushing the thought aside so much that I don't think any of us have truly understood what that means.

But Tommy is being persistent, and if there is one thing I

know about my brother, it's that when he wants something, he wants it right the fuck now.

I'm talking to him on speaker, but all the while I've also been texting Nikki. We've been talking for the past few days while Joe's been trying to figure something out with the plane tickets, and I've been enjoying how flirty our conversations have gotten.

There was a time when I thought she was adorable in every sense of the word. I've always had a soft spot for her, even before she was with Tanner. Once they started hanging out, she seemed off limits and I guess I just put her out of my mind. Now I feel bad that I all but forgot about her during our time on the road.

But there's nothing stopping me from making up for that now. I highly doubt Tanner will mind. He's been preoccupied during our whole visit, thinking more of his daughter and what he's going to do with his ex. Even when I told him that I ran into Nikki in the diner downtown, he didn't have much to say.

Sure, he seemed a little interested to hear what we talked about, but I didn't at all get the impression from him that he still has feelings for her.

"Dude, are you there? Stop wasting my fucking time and answer me!" Tommy's voice is harsh now, and I'm brought back to the moment. I finish sending a quick message back to Nikki about where she likes to hang out nowadays before answering Tommy.

"Yes, I'm here and I hear what you're saying. I still think it's a fucking stupid idea, but as long as Nikki's there to help moderate things, I guess we can give it a shot. You did tell her that we don't want the media involved, didn't you?" I ask. He confirms that he did, and I hear my phone chime once more.

It takes a lot of self-control for me to resist looking at it right away, but I know Tommy will just hang up on me if he senses me drifting again.

"Good. I don't want this to be plastered on the local news or the papers or God knows wherever else. Let's just get it done and call it good," I say.

"I want to get out of here as soon as we can. Did you talk to Greg or Joe?" Tommy asks.

I cringe slightly when I hear his plans about leaving. Of course, I know none of us were particularly eager to come here, and we were all in a rush to leave as soon as possible, but I've been having fun talking with this girl.

For the first time in a long time, I feel like I've connected with someone again, and I'm not too eager to go running off back to the lonely life I've been living. Sure, being a rock star might be the dream, but it can get awfully one-sided after a while.

"No. I thought you were taking care of that?" I ask.

He cusses under his breath. "I'm trying to, but you know how Joe is when he gets excited about sales. It's like he's forgotten that we're now three days behind and need to move on with the tour. I'm about ready to take matters into my own hands and get us the tickets myself." He sounds exasperated, and I feel my hands are tied. I'm not so eager anymore to get out of here, but I don't want him to know that. And I definitely don't want him to know why.

"I'm going to give Joe a call right now. I'll text you when I hear back from him. We'll get this figured out soon enough, but I think it's safe to say we may as well cancel the next two cities and hop straight for New York when the time comes." Tommy sighs and, for the moment, I give him my full attention.

"I don't think it'll do too much damage. We can reschedule the shows and say there was a family emergency—hopefully the fans won't be too upset." I try to sound encouraging, and I hear him chuckle on the other end of the line.

"I can guarantee you people will be upset, but shit happens. Anyway, text everyone and let them know when we're going to meet with Dad this afternoon, and let them know I expect all of them to be there." I say goodbye and assure him I'm going to.

But first, I'm going to text Nikki a little more.

As soon as I hang up the phone, I turn my attention to her messages.

Sorry, I was talking to Tommy about shit. I'm glad you guys got that visit worked out, he's stressing about everything way too much.

It's mere seconds before she replies.

I know! He seemed to be distracted when we met up yesterday. Anyway, as soon as we get this all straightened out I'm sure he'll be back to his old self

I smile. She has no idea what that even means anymore. It's been so long since she's seen him; her version of his old self and mine are two completely different things.

You mean he's going to be back to being a total asshole? I chuckle as I hit send.

Aren't all of you guys?

I love that she feels comfortable teasing me, and I smile at her flirtatiousness. As I think about how to respond, I remember how eager Tommy is to get out of town. If I want to spend more time with Nikki, then I'm just going to have to ask her out. Sooner rather than later, too.

I guess you could say that, but you love us anyway. So, do you want to grab a drink tonight? Might be a good idea to wind down after meeting with our dad this afternoon.

I stare at my phone, my hands suddenly feeling a little clammy. I can't remember the last time I felt this nervous asking a girl out, and I can't help but shake my head. I'm a rock star; it's not hard for me to find women, but when it comes to this one, I feel like a giddy schoolboy again.

Finally, I see her responding.

You know I would love to, but I already have plans with someone. Would it be possible for us to meet up tomorrow?

My heart sinks slightly. I don't know why I should be surprised. A girl as beautiful and charming as her is bound to have her pick of the lot. But if she's so eager to go out with me as soon as she's free, then I can't help but assume that whatever she's got going on tonight isn't anything too important.

Even if she's out with a guy, it can't be anything too serious if she wants to go out with me the very next day.

Hell, yeah, that works fine for me. I'll see you this afternoon then.

I hit send and sit back in my chair, only glancing down at my phone to see the smiley face she sent me. I run my hands through my hair, thinking about how much this girl has changed since the last time I saw her.

There's a part of me that can honestly see her being something permanent. A girlfriend, maybe even a wife. Sure, we've only been talking again for a couple days now, but I spent years hanging out with her almost every day. I can still see in her that little girl who used to follow my brother around like a puppy, but at the same time, she's so much more.

I flip the cap off a beer and drain it, imagining how the afternoon is going to go with my father and brothers. Part of me is glad that Nikki is going to be there. More than anything, I want her there. I almost feel like I need her to be there.

For the first time in as long as I can remember, I've got a woman on my mind and I can't get her off it.

And I don't even want to.

CHAPTER TWELVE

Tanner

"Because I totally have all the time in the world for this," I mutter under my breath as I send a quick reply to my brother. I thought we were going to be meeting with our father at the clinic this afternoon, but James sent me a second text saying that they were going to reschedule for the next day.

Since I was planning to be there to meet my ex, I didn't think it would be a big deal if I were to stay and see my father after. Now, I am going to have to come back to this godforsaken clinic and see him later.

James sends me a shitty reply, but I ignore it. I'm too high-strung to think about what they're doing, and quite honestly, I'm still more worried about seeing my daughter than anything.

A car pulls into the parking lot and I recognize my ex.

They pull up in a spot a few places down from where I'm parked, and I smile as I casually get out of the car. My heart is pounding in my chest as I round the corner, and Caitlyn stops short, Arya in her arms.

"Tanner! What are you doing here?" she snaps.

"Daddy!" Arya almost screams, throwing her arms out and struggling to be put down. Caitlyn sets her down and she runs to me, throwing her arms around me.

"I missed you so much!" I say into her long, brown hair.

"I missed you too, Daddy!" Arya cries.

Caitlyn, on the other hand, is still very clearly pissed.

"You followed me!" she snaps.

"No! I was here to visit my father but found out I couldn't see him today. I was just heading back to the car when I saw you pull in. I wasn't following you, I swear." I don't want her to do anything crazy, like take Arya away, and I'm surprised to see that she relaxes a little.

"I heard he was here. How's he doing?" she asks.

"Fine, I guess. It's hard to find the right time to see him with everyone. You look great, by the way." I turn my attention to Caitlyn fully for the first time, and I have to admit I'm somewhat surprised at what I see. She has lost all the weight she gained from her pregnancy, and she's clearly been working out.

She's as beautiful as she was when we first got together. And I can see she's clearly trying not to check me out, but she isn't doing a very good job.

"You look good yourself," she says at last.

Someone walks out of the clinic and I'm surprised to see another familiar face. Nikki appears in the parking lot, looking far better than I remember as well.

"Nikki! How good to see you," I say, giving her a light hug.

"I thought I heard a commotion out here and thought I'd come investigate," she says with a wink. I'm glad Caitlyn doesn't catch the look.

"I was just saying I was a little surprised to find him here. I didn't think I would see him again for a few more days," Caitlyn explains before adding, "Arya thought it was a wonderful surprise."

"I'm glad," Nikki says, looking from my daughter to me. It's been too long for me to be able to say I can still read her with any confidence, but I swear Nikki seems to want to hurry this along.

"Mr. Harvey is free now, if you want to get started on your session," she says to Caitlyn, who nods.

"That would be great. I do have a few things I need to take care of after my appointment." She hesitates, and I can see in her eyes that she's debating something. Finally, she squares her shoulders and holds out her hand toward Arya.

"Come on, darling, we need to go inside."

"No! I want to stay with Daddy!" Arya argues. I know this can turn out badly, so I bend down once more.

"Arya, you should go with Mommy for now. I'll see you again in a little while, okay?" I smile and give her a hug, but she starts crying.

"No, I want to stay with you! I want to stay with you!" she yells.

"Fine!" Caitlyn begrudgingly intercedes. "If you can take her for the afternoon, Tanner, I would appreciate it. But please, have her back home by five. Text me and I'll give you the address," Caitlyn says with a sigh.

I feel my heart skip a beat at this offer, and on a sudden impulse I stand up and hug her. She acts offended, but I can see a smile on her lips.

"I'm going to go get signed in. Be good for your daddy, Arya," she says, clearly wanting to get out of here before things start to really get awkward.

"I'll be right there!" Nikki calls after her. Caitlyn is already on her way inside the door, and Nikki looks at me with a wide smile.

"It sounds like you're going to have a good afternoon," she says with a wink.

"Thank you so much, Nikki," I say quietly, not wanting Arya to hear. The last thing I need is for her to tell Caitlyn that this was planned. She's not very old, but she's very smart, and it wouldn't surprise me in the least if she were to say something. "I appreciate this so much. I'm going to make it up to you, I promise!" I say.

"I can't wait to see how," Nikki replies with an open smile and a wink. I raise my eyebrows as I look at her, but she doesn't give me the chance to reply. My eyes are drawn to the sexy sway of her hips as she walks back into the clinic, but I tear them away she as she looks over her shoulder at me with another mischievous smile before disappearing out of sight.

Interesting, I think to myself. Could little Nikki Marlow still have feelings for me? I shake my head, dismissing the thought quickly. I can't assume all my exes still care for me. Besides, I hardly know Nikki well enough now to be reading too much into a simple wink. It's been a long time since we were together.

Besides, I think as I look down at my daughter, if I'm going to be getting back together with an ex, it should probably be Caitlyn. It will make everything so much *easier,* I tell myself as I take Arya's hand in my own.

We can be a family, the thought whispers in my brain.

I shake my head. *No. We can't. Some things just aren't possible.*

13

CHAPTER THIRTEEN

Nikki

BY THE TIME I'm ready to meet Tommy for drinks later this evening, I'm feeling a little on edge. There's no doubt about it, having the Bridges boys back in town is messing with my head —and my decision-making.

It was nice seeing Tanner in the parking lot earlier, but it was also much more difficult than I imagined. Any lingering feelings of jealousy and regret I thought I was feeling while we were messaging the other day came back in full force when I saw him standing there with Caitlyn and his daughter.

It didn't help that he was looking at her a bit too intensely. I thought any relationship between them was definitely over, but standing there with them, I could almost feel the tension and emotion welling up inside him over her.

And I only feel worse about the whole situation when

Caitlyn catches up with me in the hallway after her session is over.

"I just wanted to apologize for what you saw earlier in the parking lot. It's been ... a struggle, with Tanner. I know you and he used to have a thing, so I'm sure you know he isn't great with conflict." I nod in sympathy, but to be honest, I can't really relate. She keeps going, "You know, I used to think he was the man I was going to marry, but then he just left. Since Arya came along, being in contact with him ... it hasn't been easy."

She looks so sad and conflicted that I don't know what to do. Here I am, scheming behind her back and quietly lusting after her daughter's father—who also happens to my ex. Yet she's standing in front of me, pouring her heart out.

I put on my therapist hat and decided to treat it as impartially as possible. "First off, you don't have to apologize," and I mean that. "And I'm sure it's all going to work out. Clearly, you both care about Arya—and each other." My heart stings a little at that, but doing the right thing is more important than my jealousy. "It'll all work out," I say again, hoping to end the conversation before we can get into anymore detail about their relationship.

"Thank you so much, Nikki," she replies, squeezing my arm in gratitude. "That's actually very reassuring to hear. Of course, that's what my therapist says too, but it's nice hearing it from somehow who has more of a personal connection to it all," she says sincerely. I smile once more and she leaves, her step a lot lighter than it was when she walked into the building in the first place.

But the situation haunts me for the rest of my shift.

I feel caught in the middle, and I'm not sure what I even want. Yes, I want them to be happy, but what does that even mean to me? And how can I shake these weird feelings I'm having for Tanner?

And what right do I have to be jealous of the women in Tanner's life, anyway? I'm currently getting ready to meet one of his brothers for a drink, and I've spent the last few days sending flirty messages to another one of his brothers.

I know that what I'm doing probably isn't a great idea, but I just can't help myself. These Bridges men just bring something out of me that I feel has been buried under a weight of responsibility my whole life.

First it was dealing with my father, then it was trying to get through college, and now it's trying to rise in the ranks at the clinic—it feels like I've always just had one more hurdle to cross. But now, with these men back in my life, I suddenly feel so much lighter.

How am I supposed to resist that?

THE BAR TOMMY takes me to is one of the quieter ones in town. He says he wants to avoid running into any fans, and I am totally fine with that. The quiet atmosphere lends a little bit more intimacy to our conversation, and I find myself opening up a lot more than I expected.

"I just didn't know how to give the right advice to her, you know?" I look down into my beer, feeling almost silly. I told myself I wasn't going to gripe to Tommy about my day, but here we are, having a couple of drinks and talking about Caitlyn.

"Well, you and my brother were together for a while. I can imagine it makes the situation awkward for you," he says.

"I mean, we weren't together for very long. I don't know. Seeing you all back here has brought up a lot of emotions, in a way. I almost miss being a kid again," I say with a laugh. I'm relieved when he agrees.

"I hear you," he says before taking a sip of his beer. "I was really dreading coming back here, you know? This place doesn't hold too many good memories for me—or any at all, I thought. But actually being here, and seeing you, it's got me thinking that maybe living here wasn't all that bad after all." He shakes his head and gives a bit of a self-deprecating smile. I find it utterly charming.

It's not often that I've seen the big, tough Tommy Bridges vulnerable like this, and I'm surprised to find that it's a little thrilling.

"But enough of this talk of feelings," he says with a mischievous smile, "I want to know what the locals do around here for fun nowadays." He winks at me and I can feel my cheeks heat with a blush.

With the subject suitably changed, we move on to talking about all the things in the town that have changed, and what's stayed the same. And I promise myself I'm going to focus only on him for the rest of the night.

To my surprise, we end up having a wonderful time together. There is so much more to Tommy than I ever noticed when I was younger, and I wonder why I ever let our age difference get to me in the first place. He's funny and charming, and every bit as hot as I remember him being.

Tall, dark, handsome, muscular—every girl in America will be jealous of me for getting to spend my evening having drinks with him. I always thought he was more of an asshole, but tonight, I get to see a far more gentlemanly side than I ever thought possible.

"What do you say we get out of here?" he asks at last. I don't want the evening to come to an end, and there's part of me that picks up on his meaning. After a moment of hesitation, I wholeheartedly agree.

The evening has been wonderful, and I want to see where this goes.

"Let's go back to my place," I suggest with a sly grin.

. . .

I PULL my shirt over my head, completely consumed by the lust of the moment. I don't know what I thought was going to happen when I said yes to this date, but I never imagined I was going to end up having sex with Tommy Bridges.

It starts out simply. We get back to my place and I grab us a couple of beers, which we quickly finish while exchanging more small talk. Once we exhausted all our topics, I walked him to the door of my apartment. It's then that he leans in and kisses me good night, but our kiss quickly turns into something more, growing with passion.

I grab his shirt and pull him into the room, kissing him and pulling his shirt off. His hands are up my shirt in an instant, and he is kissing me with the same passion with which I am kissing him.

He runs his lips sensually up and down my neck, flicking his tongue against my skin ever so lightly. I moan and lean my head back, closing my eyes and enjoying the pleasure.

His hands are on my breasts, where they've been caressing me since my shirt fell free. Now he trails his lips down my chest, putting his face to my breasts, kissing and sucking at them, biting them. I push him back onto the couch, straddling him and biting at him as well, running my hands over his strong arms and muscular pecs.

He undoes my bra with one hand while the other runs down my back, the bite of his nails sending shivers of excitement through my entire body.

Then, he can't control himself any longer.

With a shove, he has me off him and turned around in seconds, and suddenly he's behind me. He pulls down my jeans then puts his lips to my ass, kissing me and running his hands over my tits from behind. I'm holding myself up on my knees, my hands on the couch.

I hear him unzip his jeans, and then I feel the pressure of

him teasing me from behind. We are both breathing deeply, his breaths quickening every time he pushes his massive cock against me.

"I want to be inside you so bad," he whispers. "Do you want that, baby?"

"Please, I need you inside me," I breathe. My body craves him. I can feel a yearning so deep that I know it has become a demanding need. It is then that he pushes himself inside me, and I feel him fill me to the brim.

He moans with pleasure as he slips inside, and I cry out in equal ecstasy. Slowly, Tommy begins thrusting into me, holding me still by my hips, running his hands over my body as he continues to thrust into me from behind.

I feel myself being pushed closer to orgasm with each thrust, and each time he does so, I moan and whisper words of pleasure. He's going faster and faster now, and I know he's not far behind me.

I reach around, holding his ass as he fills me, trying to take him as deep as I can. Then, I feel myself pushed over the edge, and the strongest orgasm I have felt in years overtakes me. I cry out as he surprises me by grabbing my hair and giving it a strong yank. Pleasure washes in waves over my body, and I can hardly breathe. I feel as though I'm seeing stars, and my orgasm feels like it's never going to end.

At the same time, I feel him thrust into me, hard, and at that moment his cock begins to throb. I can feel him sending his massive load deep inside me, his deep, guttural moan of pleasure pleasing me in a primal way.

We sit this way for a few moments, him lightly rocking behind me as his hands continue to explore my body, me basking in his attention, neither of us speaking. Then he pulls himself out of me, leaving me feeling incredibly satisfied.

"That was incredible, Tommy," I breathe as he pulls up his

jeans. He gives me a mischievous look and slaps my ass as I stand, and I squeal with delight.

He doesn't stay the night, but I'm okay with that. This evening is more than I ever could have asked for, and I'm glad that I agreed to go out with him. But I don't expect this to go anywhere—it's an enjoyable night that ends with even more enjoyable sex.

It's taken my mind off my muddled feelings about Tanner, and in a way, it gives me hope. Now, it doesn't seem to matter if nothing happens with Tanner, and I feel I can handle that possibility better.

After all, I am a strong, desirable woman. I am in control of my life.

I can handle whatever comes my way.

CHAPTER FOURTEEN

Tommy

"Let's get this show on the road." It's a phrase I've said for as long as I can remember, and my brothers always get a kick out of teasing me about it. Today, however, it seems to do nothing but bring more tension into the situation.

"We get it. We're moving," Janus snaps. He's hungover, so I don't do anything but roll my eyes at him. He knew we were going to go see Dad today. He shouldn't have gone out the night before.

Tanner seems to be in the best spirits out of all of us, and I can only imagine it has something to do with his kid. Nathan and James, on the other hand, are in just as foul a mood as I am.

"I just want to keep this as short as possible," Nathan says as we walk into the clinic.

"Don't we all," James replies tartly.

"Hello!" Nikki interrupts the conversation as she walks

around the corner, and we all instinctively stiffen. "I hope you're all well this morning!" She makes eye contact with me very briefly before moving on to take in the rest of my brothers. "If you come this way, I'll take you to the visitor center."

"A lot better now that we get to see you," James says, and Nikki giggles. I raise my eyebrow, glancing between the two. We've all been flirty with Nikki since getting here, but there's something between them that makes me wonder if there's a bit more at play there. And in a way, I can almost imagine she's ignoring me.

We haven't texted this morning, and didn't say much about the sex other than to say how amazing it was—and it definitely was—before I left her place last night. Still, I would expect her to be a little more welcoming to all of us—not just James.

I don't have much time to think about this, however, as she opens the door and the three of us step into the visitor center. Our father is sitting next to one of the tables, looking a lot worse than I thought he would. I feel a pang run through my chest, and a whole series of new emotions run through me.

"Boys!" he calls out when we get near him. I grimace, watching as he slowly rises.

"How good to see you! I was nervous you wouldn't show!" He moves through all of us, shaking our hands and giving us hugs.

It's clear that none of us are at ease in this situation, and Nikki does her best to make the interaction go as smoothly as possible.

"I've been visiting your father for a few months now, almost like his unofficial therapist, and you might say we've gotten rather close," she says with a smile.

"Hopefully not too close," Janus snaps. She gives him a look, and the rest of us pretend not to have heard what he said.

"He's been talking about seeing you since we heard you were

going to come through here," Nikki continues. Several of my brothers exchange looks, and I shift from one foot to the other.

"I thought we were coming through here because you wanted us to," Nathan says. He raises his eyebrows, looking at our father with an accusatory stare. Dad looks at him first, then at the rest of us, and I can see the confusion in his face.

"If I knew it was that easy, then I would have asked you all to come a long time ago," he says with a hoarse laugh.

"It was you? I was under the impression it was the clinic that asked us to come. Was this all a grand plan for you to see me again, Nikki?" James asks as he turns to her once more. He puts on his best grin, the one I've see him use on countless women at countless bars, and I see her blush.

I can't help but shake my head. In the back of my mind, I want to tell him to lay off. He's trying too hard. Then there's another part of me that wants to turn around and walk out.

If it weren't for me, none of us would be here. This certainly isn't easy on any of us, so why the fuck is Nikki going to get any of the credit?

"I talked to the clinic a little while ago, and they said you weren't doing very well, Dad. That's why we're here. If you've followed our career at all, then you know we have an album out right now that's doing very well. We thought we would put on a couple of shows while we were in the area." I change the subject back to us, hoping that our father will, for once in his life, care about something that's going on in our lives.

"Very nice. I have been keeping up with you, as much as Nikki is able to tell me, at least. You can imagine it's difficult for me to get online or do anything like that myself these days. But I'm glad to hear that you're able to turn this into something profitable while you're here." He smiles once more, but his words sting.

"Oh yes, of course you'd bring up profit, Dad," Janus replies.

"As I recall, you were doing your best to get in on the profit when we were just starting out. Or is that something I'm not remembering properly?"

"I did no such thing! I did nothing but support you from the beginning. I sacrificed so much for the lot of you!" Our father is clearly growing upset, but now I am getting pissed off as well.

I remember what our childhood was like, and if it wasn't for me stepping up, none of my brothers would have had the kind of childhood they did.

James remembers the problems Dad had with alcohol, too, and the way he used to treat us. Dad has some serious gaps in his memory if he thinks he is a martyr.

"Is that why you drowned yourself in a bottle of Jack every night?" The words are out of my mouth before I have the chance to stop them, and I can see the rage come into my father's face. It's a familiar look, and one that I hoped I would never see again.

"You know what?" he fairly shouts, but before he has the chance to say anything else, Nikki intervenes.

"All right, I think that is enough for this visit. That was good. I'm glad you were all able to make it, and I'm glad you got to see your sons. But it's getting to be time for you to take your medication." She puts her hands on his shoulders, looking down at him with a smile.

The look she gives us lets us know it's our cue to leave. Though all my brothers are trying to calm the situation down, telling my dad it is good to see him, I turn on my heel and leave. I walk right out of the clinic, not caring if I ever come back or see him again.

The meeting didn't go well at all, and it makes me regret ever coming back to this stupid fucking town. I hear my brothers behind me in the hall, James calling out one last thing to Nikki as he trails along at the back of the group.

I shake my head, heading back to the rental car. I don't care which of them decides to drive, but I'm going to sit and stew, staring out the window. I wish so many things about my life were different, and I thought being back home, I could make some of those things happen.

But as we pull out of the parking lot of the clinic, I can't help but shake my head.

Some things are never going to change.

15

CHAPTER FIFTEEN

Nikki

I HAVE TO ADMIT, I am looking forward to the night out with James. Though I woke up after my night with Tommy thinking it'd be best to cancel my plans with James, my intentions changed drastically after the disastrous meeting with their father.

I expected it to be tense, but I can't believe how it all went down. I am somewhat embarrassed when I put the poor man back in his room.

"They hate me!" he says after the meeting. I can't tell if he's angry or sad, but I argue.

"No, they don't, they're just confused," I try. He insists that they hate him, and I have to give him his medication to calm him down. I wish there was something else I could say or do for him, but after spending a few more minutes with him, trying to get his mind off it all, I have to move on with my day.

I consider reaching out to James or Tommy, but I don't know what to say that might help smooth things over. Eventually I decide to just get back to work and deal with it later.

However, it's not long after the brothers leave that James starts texting me, cheerfully thanking me for arranging the meeting and telling me he's looking forward to our drinks tonight.

James, I'm so sorry! I thought the meeting would be great for all of you, but I don't think that could have gone much worse! Did you see how he and Tommy got in each other's faces?

I wait for the reply, and am surprised at how casual he is.

They've done that for as long as I can remember. I wouldn't worry about it. But enough about that. Tell me what you're going to be wearing to our date later.

He ends the text with a winking emoji, and I shake my head at his enthusiasm, smiling all the while. After seeing James this morning, I haven't really been able to get him out of my mind.

He's charming, to say the least, but there's something else there, too. Something that makes me even more drawn to him than I thought possible. But I don't want to dwell on it too much.

In fact, I try very hard not to dwell on it. Just as I try even harder not to dwell on the fact that I had mind-blowing sex with his brother just last night.

The brothers are already in the middle of some intense family drama, and the very last thing I want to do is cause any more issues. But I've been starved for attention from them for so long that I can't make clearheaded decisions when it comes to them.

Should I tell James about Tommy? *No*, my gut tells me emphatically. Last night with Tommy was just a one-time thing. There's no need to be getting these brothers angry at one another—not that I think Tommy will get all that mad about it.

He seems to be on the same page as me when it comes to the casualness of our night.

And besides, they'll all be leaving soon anyway. I might as well enjoy my time with them while they're here.

So I'll go for drinks with James, not mention anything about my night with Tommy, and I'll keep my clothes *on* this time. Probably.

With that sorted out, I get back to focusing on work.

After all, I've got other things to do.

"You look amazing," James says with a smile as he picks me up later that night. I'm wearing a tight T-shirt and a short skirt, embracing one of my favorite looks from high school.

"So do you," I say. He always wears the same jeans and T-shirt sort of look, and he always pulls it off. He looks incredible tonight, as he always does.

I look him over, feeling a surge of lust take over me. I tamp it down as quickly as I can, and I ignore it for the moment as we head out to the bar.

As James talks about his favorite parts of being in the band and keeps me laughing all night with stories from on the read, I feel a connection to him again that I felt earlier at the clinic. While I know there is something between us, I'm surprised at how strongly I'm drawn to him.

I realize suddenly that I won't be able to stick to my previous resolve, and know that I have to be honest with him as well. And when he presents me with the opportunity, I know I have to fess up.

"So, your plans last night must not have been too great if you're out here with me tonight," he says with a wink and charming grin that makes me blush.

I've never blushed as much in my life as I have today with him. Something about him makes me feel light and giddy, and I want to be as honest with him as I can be—without causing more drama between him and his family.

"I went out for drinks with someone. It was a good time, actually," I reply lamely. I watch him as I speak, hoping that he's not deterred. He doesn't seem to be, and he looks at me with a sly grin of his own.

"You're pretty popular, aren't you?" he teases.

I blush again.

"It's a small town. You know how it goes." So, being honest with him is a bit more difficult than I imagined, and I'm now hoping that the subject changes as quickly as possible.

"All too well," he says as he rolls his eyes, and I sigh in relief.

We continue to chat and drink the night away, and just as I felt last night with Tommy, I never want it to end.

Man, do I really have a weakness for these Bridges men.

"You ever been on a real tour bus?" he asks later in the evening, and I laugh and shake my head.

"Do I look like someone who would need a tour bus?" I ask him with a twinkle in my eye. He looks me over, pretending to analyze me, and then shrugs.

"Well, regardless, I think you would like to see a real tour bus," he says. I toss my hair back and give him a sly smile.

"Hmm, is that what you think?" I pause for dramatic effect, already knowing what my answer will be. At this point, with him staring at me with his laughing, sparkling eyes, I'm feeling pretty helpless to deny him anything.

"All right, then, why don't you show me your real tour bus?"

He makes an elaborate bow and holds out his hand.

"Come with me, my dear, and your wish is my command."

. . .

As soon as we enter the bus, he grabs my arm, spinning me around to face him. I hardly have a second to question my decision-making abilities before we begin kissing, our mouths hungry for each other. His mouth is pressed firmly against mine, our tongues are exploring each other. I'm moaning, allowing the quiet sounds to escape as we continue to make out, our hands exploring each other's bodies.

He reaches under my skirt and grabs my ass, pulling me into him. I can feel that he's already hard, and it sends a thrill of excitement through me.

I push him down on the bench seat and kneel between his legs. I lift his shirt up just a little, so I can kiss his muscled belly as I start to undo his pants. I gasp lightly as his cock springs into my hands as soon as his zipper is down—he isn't wearing anything beneath his jeans.

I take him in my mouth, looking up into his eyes as I do. He leans back, closing his eyes and shuddering at the sensation of my warm, wet mouth. I flick my tongue around the head of his cock then run it down the length of his shaft, feeling my own pussy grow wetter with each move I make.

He reaches down, rubbing his fingers between my legs. My short skirt leaves nothing to the imagination, and he's easily able to slide his fingers under my panties and inside me. When lust overtakes me and I can't ignore it any longer, I stand up, sliding my panties off and letting them fall free.

I get on top of him, positioning his cock at my wet entrance and sitting down slowly, feeling his massive dick disappear inside me. A moan escapes my lips and he shudders once more at the tightness of my pussy surrounding him.

I put my hands on his shoulders and begin to ride, looking into his sparkling eyes in the pale light as I do.

I'm riding him faster now, and each time I rise and fall on his dick I feel him pushing me closer and closer to climax. I'm riding him as fast as I can, moaning with pleasure, not bothering to keep my voice down in the empty bus.

When he reaches down to start fingering my clit, I feel my orgasm begin to overtake me, and I moan with satisfaction. I continue to ride him, sending a new wave through me with each thrust. It's intense, and I know I'm not going to have the strength to continue once my climax ends.

James must realize this as well, as he begins to help me, holding me in place on his lap as he pumps himself into me. I feel him thrust into me, hard, and he cries out as he cums. I can feel his dick jump inside me, emptying his load deep inside my wet pussy.

I sit on his lap, my head resting against his shoulder as I feel him go soft inside me. I'm holding him close to my body, and his face is nestled in my breasts. I caress the back of his head, enjoying the moment for all that it is. I don't want to sever this connection, don't want this to end, but I know it has to.

I don't know how long has passed when I finally lift my head from his shoulder. It may have been ten minutes or two hours for all I knew. But at last, I rise, feeling the warmth of him run down my leg as I do so. I quickly pull up my panties.

I pull down my skirt and he pulls up his jeans, the two of us looking at each other like naughty schoolchildren. We laugh as we step out of the bus, and James offers to take me home.

Before he opens the car door for me, he lightly pins me against the side of the car, giving me a short but intense kiss. When he releases my mouth, he pulls back and looks me in the eyes, a secret smile on his lips.

"I hope this compares favorably to last night's," he says with a wink, his sly grin still in place.

My heart stops for a moment, wondering for the first time if Tommy might have told James about our night together.

When I don't say anything, he laughs and kisses me again.

"That's all right, sweetheart, a little competition won't scare me away." He winks again before releasing me and opening my door.

The ride to my place is pretty quiet, filled with small touches and glances here and there. As I climb the stairs to my apartment, I can't help but replay the night and compare it to last night, now that James has put that thought in my head.

I had a lot of fun with both him and Tommy, but there is something deeper about sex with James. If he'd simply put on his pants and left with hardly any word, as Tommy did, I definitely would've felt hurt. I didn't feel hurt in the least when Tommy did that.

There is certainly a greater connection between James and I, and I can't help but wonder if there might be something more there. He all but declared that he will fight for me, but do I want that? I shake my head, pushing the thought out of my mind.

They're all going to be leaving soon. Why should I expect their leaving this time to be any different from the last? They'll probably leave and never look back again.

I've been spending the whole day worrying about hurting the brothers, but I suddenly realize that I don't want to get hurt by any of the brothers again, either. If I start imagining these connections between us and entertaining thoughts of a future with one of them, then I'm afraid that very thing might happen.

I'll just take life as it comes, and leave it at that.

And I'll enjoy the ride while it lasts.

CHAPTER SIXTEEN

Tanner

"I THOUGHT you'd really changed this time, Tanner, but now you're making me think I must be an idiot to have ever felt that way!" Caitlyn hangs up the phone before I have the chance to say anything else, and I sigh.

I want to call her back and tell her that she's not an idiot, that it's just a mistake. I want to tell her that I'm feeling tense from how the meeting went with my father the day before. But I still don't feel like I can really open up to her.

In a way, she's right. I haven't changed. In many ways, I'm in the same place I was when we were together, and that doesn't bode well, considering the way I ended things.

I know I must not have changed much if I'm thinking about asking her to pursue another relationship with me. Despite the difficult years we've had, being in the same city as her this past week has made me realize that I'm just as drawn to her now as I ever was. But I know if there's any hope for us, then I'm going to have to be more of a teammate than I have been in the past.

The problem with that is it's much more difficult than it sounds. I don't like opening up to anyone.

It feels strange, not wanting to hang out with her or my daughter. I want to see Arya more than anything, but I don't really want to deal with the emotions that come with seeing Caitlyn. Not today. So I had to cancel our plans. I'll make sure I spend more time with her before we leave.

But even the thought of leaving has a pang running through my heart.

Suddenly, I have an idea. I pick up my phone and shoot a quick text to Nikki. James gave her number out to everyone, and though I tried to argue that it wasn't a good idea at first, he convinced me that we might want to get a hold of Dad through Nikki.

Now, I'm glad he was so insistent.

Hey, I thought I might make good on my promise and take you out to dinner tonight. I do really appreciate what you did for me.

I hit send, wondering how long it's going to be before she accepts, hoping her response isn't too enthusiastic. After our brief meeting in the parking lot of the clinic, I figured she must still have feelings for me, though I can't imagine why. We had fun when we dated back in high school, but it was never all that serious.

I thought our breakup was mutual, that we both realized we made better friends than romantic partners.

Even as I think of any lingering feelings she might have for me, I remember how painfully obvious it was to all of us that she and James were flirting with each other over the meeting with our dad. I wonder if even Dad picked up on it. Granted, the meeting didn't last long before he and Tommy were going at it, as always, but there was certainly enough flirting going on to catch our attention.

My phone chimes and I pick it up, but my heart sinks.

Thanks for the sweet offer, but you really don't have to. I've got a lot going on tonight. Maybe we can try for another time?

I look at my phone for a moment, not realizing how excited I was at the prospect of seeing her until it was taken off the table. I can't help but wonder what she's doing. I always had trouble reading her, thinking she was just the kind of girl to run hot and cold. One minute I thought she was planning our wedding, then the next I felt that she only wanted a fling for the school year and then she'd be on to someone else.

But this feels strange, and I want to get to the bottom of it.

You know, I think I would really like to take you out tonight, if you can manage. I don't want to pressure you, but it's been a while and I'd love to catch up. Let me know if your plans change tonight.

Aside from trying to solve the mystery that is Nikki Marlow, I really do mean it. Being back in this town has made me remember how very supportive Nikki always was. She was probably the only true friend any of us had while growing up here, and I want to reconnect with that feeling.

Of course, I don't know exactly what she wants from me, after our brief encounter in the parking lot, and I'll be careful with her. I won't say or do anything that could possibly get back to Caitlyn—not that I think Nikki is the kind of girl to do something like that to me.

When she declines a second time, I'm about to give up. She seemed so excited by the prospect of getting together before, but I don't want to play games with anyone today, and I don't want to waste anymore mental energy trying to figure out anyone else's motivations. If she's changed her mind and doesn't want to go out with me, that's fine, but I'm not going to be made the bad guy again when she gets butthurt that I left.

Suddenly, I have another idea.

All right, I guess I can't force you to hang out with me if you don't want to, lol, but keep in mind that we'll be leaving any day now, and I don't know when we're going to be back through again. I would really like to take you out before we go, and I can't promise that I'll be able to do it after tonight.

I hit send and wait, deciding I'm not going to let her answer ruin my night. I can see she's typing, and I fully expect her to turn me down once more.

But I'm surprised by her response.

That's true. Besides, this can wait, I guess. I'm just feeling guilty that I haven't been working as much as I was before you guys got to town, but work can wait. Let's do it!

She sends me several smiley faces, and I smile to myself. There are some things that haven't changed about her, and that is one of them. Even though I don't want anything from her but a platonic friendship, I can appreciate that she still has some of the same qualities that attracted me to her when we dated in high school.

Great! I knew you would come around to my way of thinking. When do you want me to pick you up?

I send her a winking emoji, hoping that I'm not coming off as too flirty. I miss the times she and I had together, but that doesn't mean that I want them back. She is quick to respond this time, telling me she gets off work around five and would like an hour to get ready before we head out.

I agree and she sends me the address to her apartment, and I set my phone down. At first, I have the urge to text Caitlyn and tell her I want to make plans with her the following night, but I resist.

Though I have never spent much time thinking about why I felt the need to leave that relationship, I can't help but feel that part of the problem was that we were forcing something when there shouldn't have been a need for any force.

Caitlyn wanted more than I wanted to give at that time, and the way she went about telling me only drove me farther away. I fear now that if I do the same thing to her, or if I do it for the wrong reason, then she's going to pull back entirely. Not only will that ruin any chance I have with her, but it will ruin any other chance I have of seeing Arya while I'm here.

I know I have a lot of things to work out in my head before I mention anything to Caitlyn. Being back home has made me realize how much I truly do want a family—but I want a better one than I ever had growing up. And I want that for Arya too.

But I know it won't be fair to either of them if I try to pursue something with Caitlyn just because it looks easier on paper. If I do want to try again with Caitlyn, it needs to be because of Caitlyn.

As I start sorting out what I'm going to wear out tonight when I meet up with Nikki, I realize that it's about time to get some laundry done. For all their faults, my brothers have all done a better job of keeping up with their laundry. I've been sporting the same shirts multiple days in a row.

With a sigh, I start shoving my dirty laundry in my backpack and grab my headphones. I'll hang out down at the laundry while I wait. The last thing I need is for some punk kid to run off with my wash when I'm here in the hotel waiting for it to get done.

I slip my key into the lock and head out into the hall, refusing to let my mind imagine what it would be like to have a place with Caitlyn. The more I think about it, the more I want it, and rationally, I know that that reality is actually a longshot.

All I can do is try.

CHAPTER SEVENTEEN

Nikki

I CHECK myself over in the mirror once more, trying not to be overly critical. My body has changed in many ways since high school, many for the better, but some not so much. I have to admit to myself that I'm never going to weigh what I did then, but at the same time I can't be too critical of that—the price I pay in weight comes with an incredible ass and boobs that would make Dolly herself jealous.

I don't know why I feel so nervous. This is Tanner. I've known him for years, have dated him, and felt that I'd moved on. Until just a few days ago, he was just another name on the list of exes I had, and I never gave him much thought besides. At least, no more thought than I gave to any of the Bridges brothers.

Now I can't get him out of my mind. I can't get any of them out of my mind. Anytime I'm with one of them, they're all I can think about. When I'm alone, they all take up space in my head.

James flashes through once more, as does Tommy. I haven't spoken to Tommy much since the night he and I went out, and I am wondering how he's feeling about the way that night ended.

I thought he would say something about it the next day, but with the way things went with his father, he and I never got the chance to speak. I was also surprised that he never bothered to text me later that afternoon. I thought about texting him, but figured he might not want to hear from me just then, so decided to leave the ball in his court.

I push it all out of my mind now as I hear the car pull up in front of my apartment. A quick glance outside tells me it's Tanner, and I hurry to put on the final touches to my makeup.

"Hey! Nice ride," I tease as I slide into the front seat of the rental.

"It was all they had, and I couldn't say no. Nathan and Janus took the other car downtown. I don't even want to know what kind of trouble they're planning on getting into tonight." He rolls his eyes and we head off toward the restaurant.

I worry that we aren't going to have enough to talk about, but I'm surprised when the conversation takes off.

"How has your life been? If you pay any attention at all you know what I've been up to," he says with a laugh. I laugh and shake my head.

"Between work and college, and now even more work, I didn't keep tabs on you after we broke up. Not much, anyway." I give him a mischievous look and he laughs.

"And here I thought all my exes fawned over me until they had the chance to see me again," he teases. Then he looks at me with a more serious look in his eyes. "Honestly, though, I'm surprised no one has snatched you up yet. I thought you wanted to settle down with someone."

"I did, but I would rather settle down with the right one than just anyone, you know? I'll admit that it's been harder to find the one than I thought it was going to be." I laugh and he joins in, nodding his head in agreement.

We get to the restaurant and are seated immediately, and I'm further surprised to learn he had reservations.

"I wanted to make sure we got a table. Like I said, you never know when we're going to be sent off again, and I didn't want to miss the chance to say thanks." He shifts nervously in his seat, and I raise my eyebrows.

"How are things going with Caitlyn, if you don't mind me asking?"

"Fine. Good, actually, for the most part. I have to say I'm surprised. She's been a lot better than I thought she would be, and I ... I don't know." I can tell there's so much more he wants to say, but there's something holding him back. I feel that odd tinge of jealousy rising in my chest once more, but I dive for my drink, doing everything I can to make it go away, or to at least hide it.

"Would it be crazy if she and I were to get back together?" he blurts out suddenly. I look at him in surprise, raising my eyebrows.

"What do you mean?" I ask.

"The other day, Arya asked me if it would be possible for us to be a family. I don't know. She wants me in her life, but not like I am. She wants us to be a real family." He's looking down at his drink, and I can't help but wonder how long he's been carrying this around.

"I don't think it would be weird. I just hope it would work," I volunteer. I don't want to throw a damper on his dream, but I do want him to be realistic. "I mean, can you imagine what it would be like if you and I were to get back together?" I don't know why I say it, but I want to see his reaction.

It's not something he's ever hinted at—hell, we've hardly

even talked since we broke up—but the thought has obviously crossed my mind a few times since he came back to town.

I've even questioned my attraction to his brothers, thinking that I might just be trying to substitute any Bridges brother for the one I really want. But my brain immediately dismisses that idea, especially as I think back on how great both of my nights were with Tommy and James.

But to know that he would consider getting back with Caitlyn just makes me wonder if he would ever consider such a thing with me, and makes me wonder just how strong his feelings are for Caitlyn. He laughs, and I feel my heart sink briefly, but I am soon able to laugh about it as well.

"No, I really can't. What you and I had was certainly special, but I don't think you and I are anything like the people we were then. I don't think something between us now would be a good thing for either of us." He shakes his head with another laugh, and I nod.

A part of me hates to agree—nobody likes hearing rejection—but I have to. I don't like these nostalgic feelings in my heart, but I can't help them. They're blinding me to my true feelings and the reality of my situation—and they're like a combination of sadness, jealously, and naiveté all wrapped up into one.

It's not a good feeling.

We get through dinner, chatting away like old friends. He tells me about the tattoo shop he's been running in the town he's currently living in, and I tell him as many funny stories as I can about work without giving away any particular details about the patients.

I'm amazed at how much better we are together without romance getting in the way. That is, until we get to the car. Tanner walks around the front of the car and opens the door for me, but before I step inside, he leans forward and presses his lips to mine.

Though it takes me by surprise, I don't miss a beat, and I kiss him back, our passion growing as our arms wrap around each other. I can feel myself burning with a desire to have him, and I wonder what's going through his mind. There's no doubt that his kiss is hot, but there isn't the same flame to it that I had with either of his brothers.

Then, all at once, he pulls away. Standing on the other side of the door, he smiles as I slip inside. I don't know if he's sorry for the kiss, or if I should be, or what he's even thinking. He walks back around the front of the car and gets in the driver's seat, looking at me with a strange look in his eyes.

"I don't know why, but I just needed to do that," he says after a few moments of silence. He doesn't apologize, and I can feel all the emotions that I thought I'd just gotten over trying to peek their pesky little heads up again. But there's a stronger feeling settling in too. Something that tells me we're better off as friends and nothing more.

The drive back to my apartment is filled with a bit of idle chatter, and I'm relieved that it's not going to be awkward between us.

I still feel an annoying pang when he doesn't get out of the car. I'm starting to think my ego needs a check, if there's still a part of me that was hoping he would follow me up to my place. Maybe this rejection from him is good for me, in the long run

He doesn't get out, of course. He just sits with a smile on his face and thanks me for joining him for dinner, and once again thanks me for making it possible for him to reconnect with his daughter.

"You know I would do anything for you," I say as I lean in toward the window. He nods.

"You are one in a million," he replies with a smile that melts my heart. I pat the door where the window is rolled down, and then turn to go inside. He lingers for a moment before driving away, but I keep my eyes on my building, refusing to look back.

As I enter my apartment, there are a lot of feelings flowing through me. I feel a little foolish—everyone likes to believe that their ex would take them back in a heartbeat, given the chance, and it's a real blow to know that I was living in that fantasy world. But I also feel a sense of peace and closure that I didn't realize I was missing.

I know now, without a doubt, that he and I aren't going to get back together, and that's okay. I don't have to spend anymore time thinking about what might've been. Though there is a small pang of hurt—mostly hurt pride, I'll admit—I'm almost rooting for him and Caitlyn to get back together.

I would love to see her happy, and I would love for little Arya to grow up with the father she deserves.

But more than anything, I want to see Tanner happy.

I really, truly do.

CHAPTER EIGHTEEN

Tommy

Finally, the knocking at my door stops. I roll over in my bed, draping my hand over my forehead. I have done everything I know of to get rid of this hangover, but for some reason, this is one that just won't be shaken.

Nathan has been trying to get me out of bed for a couple hours, first by blowing up my phone then by knocking on the door to my room. I've told him to fuck off more than once, and I feel bad that I have to be so rude to him, but I don't want to deal with any of the fuckers.

They're able to handle themselves just fine in life, right up until the moments I really don't want to be bothered. Then, the next thing I know, they're all over me, trying to find out what I'm doing or what I need.

I need to be fucking left alone.

The first few days in town were a whirlwind of emotion for

me. I thought that I hated it here, but so many things came rushing back that made me question how much I hated it, and how much I really just didn't want to remember.

Then Nikki came into the picture. I didn't know what to make of her, or how I felt about her. She's drop-dead gorgeous; of course I noticed that right away, but I didn't have any idea what I wanted with her, at first.

In a way, she is like a drug. She is an escape from the darkness I feel in this town. But she is also the one thing that makes me connect with my father once more, and that leaves me feeling broken.

That feeling of brokenness is the same feeling I had when I left town the first time, and it is the same feeling that is taking me over now.

I got drunk the night before, seeking to forget all about the interaction with my father. In fact, there was part of me that questioned whether I was trying to forget that I even had a father in the first place.

Now that I'm sober, I have to face the facts of my life again, and I really don't want to. I'm too old and have too many things to do to get drunk again. Plus, it's only ten in the morning. I'm not Janus, after all. I'll leave the day drinking to him.

My phone chimes and I sigh. I'm ready to send Nathan the most scathing message I can come up with, but I'm surprised to see that text is actually from Nikki.

Hey, it's been a few days since I've heard from you. Just wanted to check in before you guys hit the road.

I smile to myself. It's nice to know that someone cares about me, without having any familial obligation compelling them to do so.

I don't know what to say to her, though. Part of me wants to open up to her and share with her exactly how I'm feeling, like I was able to that night when we out, but another part of me wants to blow her off with the rest of the world.

I'm fine. Not thrilled with how things went with Dad, but fine. What can I expect? Some people are never going to change, and I don't know why the fuck I thought he would.

There's silence for a few moments, and I begin to wonder if she's pissed that I got in his face like I did. I'm not sorry about it in the slightest. I'm sorry that I didn't tell him more about how I felt. I'm sorry that I let it go this long, only to have that happen to me all over again. But am I sorry that I got in his face in front of everyone?

Fuck, no, I'm not.

My phone chimes again, and I snatch it from the bed, scanning the message.

Not to go all therapist on you, but this might be something you should talk to someone about in person. What do you say we meet up this afternoon over a cup of coffee and we can talk about it? Not how your father is, but how you are feeling about things. It might help.

I feel a twinge in my heart, and I'm not sure what it is I'm feeling. I appreciate that she cares, but opening up to anyone has never been easy for me. I don't need a therapist. If I did, I would have gotten one a long time ago.

But then, Nikki's more than a therapist. She's a friend who cares about all of us—who cares about my family—and I know she's not going to judge me or tell me anything that wouldn't be for the good of the situation. So I agree.

Now, with a reason to get out of bed, I throw my feet to the floor. I groan as I sit up, wondering why I can't drink like I used to. I don't recall when this happened. It's like I was fine one night, having no problem throwing back beer after beer, then the next night I was sick as a dog if I looked at alcohol the wrong way.

I get up and get dressed, but as I'm shaving, my phone rings.

Thinking it's Nikki, I pick it up and answer without looking at the caller ID.

"Hello?"

"Tommy? Good God, man, you sound like death itself."

I recognize the voice but look down at my phone anyway. It's Joe.

"It was a rough night. What do you want?" I ask impatiently.

"I need you to go down to the shop and look at the bus. I don't understand a single word fucking Javier says to me, and I'm not going to trust Greg with that. Get back to me when you know what's up."

I roll my eyes. Of course today would be the day I have to go play mechanic.

"What the fuck, Joe? They still don't have the part in there?" I snap.

"You're acting once again like this is my fucking fault, when I'm the only one who's been trying to get you guys out of there," he replies dryly.

"As I recall, you are the one who decided putting on a show here would be a good idea," I remind him.

He changes the subject immediately. "Anyway, get down there and see what you think, then get back to me. Once I know what's going on, then we can move forward."

"Fucking A," I reply and hang up. Now I'm going to have to bail on Nikki, which I really don't want to do.

Hey, sweetheart, it turns out the fuckhead I work for needs me to get down to the mechanic. Let's meet up another time, all right?

I set my phone down, dragging the razor over my face. When the phone chimes once more, I pick it up, hoping she argues with me.

She doesn't.

Oh no! I hope you guys get that fixed soon, but it sounds good anyway. Get a hold of me when you're free. I really want to see you again before you go!

I sigh. I don't know what kind of reply I was hoping for, but it wasn't that. I set down my razor and type a quick reply.

For sure.

I hit send and force her from my mind.

CHAPTER NINETEEN

James

"WE'RE GOING to have to make a decision soon. You know how Joe is. He loves to wait until the last second to tell us something, and that doesn't give us a lot of time to fix it." I know I don't have to tell Tommy this, but I'm more venting my frustration to him than I am informing him.

He nods. I can see in his face he's just as frustrated with the situation as I am, but he's still feeling tense about what happened the other day with our father. There's more on his plate than mine, and in a way I feel sorry for him.

"Joe was telling me this morning he didn't think we were going to have to wait much longer, but then Javier seems to think that the bus is going to be down and out for another week at least." Tommy shakes his head. I didn't go to the mechanic shop with him, so he's the one who knows how bad it actually is.

"So what does he want us to do?" I ask. I'm almost afraid to hear the answer, but I know we're going to have to face the facts sooner or later.

"I called and talked to him for nearly an hour, discussing all our options. The bottom line is really that we need to move forward with the tour and come back for the bus when it's fixed. If we get plane tickets, we won't have to worry so much about the timeline." He's staring at the floor of his room as he speaks, and I sit down on the bed.

"Does he have the money to finance that? I hope he realizes we've been living off our own money since we got here, and this hotel wasn't cheap after the first few days were up." I'm more frustrated about the thought of leaving than I am about the plane tickets, but if I'm going to be forced to go then he damn well better have the tickets ready.

"He said he already had the money on the way, and we just need to get the tickets when we can. If we book now, we can be out of here and on our way by this weekend, which is, honestly, most ideal. You know as well as I do that we can't fuck this up with the record label, or we're going to be right back to square one." Tommy is talking, but we aren't looking at each other.

I nod. He's right, after all. We've worked too long and too hard to get to where we are with this album; we can't fuck it up with the fans by blowing off anymore shows.

But there's something about the way he's talking about this situation that makes me think he might not be so eager to leave, either.

"What is it?" I ask after a moment of silence.

"What?"

"Come on, you know I can read you pretty well. You don't want to leave here anymore than I do, what is it?" I prompt. He gives me a look.

"Why don't *you* want to leave?" he snaps. I cringe. I'm not prepared for that question, and I sigh.

"Is it Dad or is it Nikki?" I ask.

He raises his eyebrows. "Give me more credit than that. I know you guys went out together a couple times, and I could see the way you were looking at her when we showed up to meet with Dad. There has to be something there."

I look him dead in the eyes, wanting to know the answer for a few different reasons, but he laughs.

"You mean when you were flirting with her like a lovestruck schoolboy? What the fuck man? That was embarrassing for all of us!" He shakes his head with a smirk, and I know he's trying to get a rise out of me.

I push my anger aside, wanting to know the truth.

"Are you sure it's her you want, or is it just what you think she can do for us?" I ask. He gives me another look with raised eyebrows, and I continue. "I mean, she did make it sound like she was going to fix things between us and Dad. I'm not going to lie, I thought that would've been pretty awesome, actually." I've never said anything like this to him before, but I can see in his face that he agrees.

We don't want to admit it, not even to each other, but we do want to have that relationship with our father. We just want to have a relationship that works for us as well as him.

"I don't know, man. There is a lot of fucking confusion that comes with that girl. She's so different than I remember her, but you could be right. I don't know how the fuck I feel about anything anymore. And I think we have this fucking town to thank for it." Tommy shakes his head and starts pacing back and forth, and I feel a measure of relief wash over me.

"I know what you mean. It's like being back brought up all the good about growing up here, but a hell of a lot of the bad, too," I reply.

He nods, and there are a few more seconds of silence between us. At last, he changes the subject.

"I think the best thing to do is to get the guys together and tell them that we're going to be moving out. We can't stay here and piss all our money away while we wait for that piece of shit bus to get fixed. We have a career to focus on, first and foremost." He claps his hands together and I nod, though I don't want to agree.

But he's right. We can't live in this fantasy forever, and we do have an album to promote. No one is going to be happy about having to leave, but then, that's the life of a rock star—always on the move.

Until we came back here, no one thought they'd ever want to step foot in this town again. We aren't going to throw a fit because we have to leave.

"I'll send out a round of texts," I say as I get up off the bed, and Tommy nods.

"I'll get a hold of Joe and see what he wants us to do as far as the tour goes. He's going to have more information for me on the next city. We'll aim to be out of here by the end of the weekend." I nod as I walk out of the room, closing the door behind me.

But once I'm in the hallway, I hesitate to send out the texts. I'm going to do it, but I want to give myself a minute to think about what Tommy said, and how I feel about this situation.

He all but said that Nikki was nothing more than a distraction to him, but I've also always had difficulty reading him at times. I could swear that I saw something between them when they were together in that hospital room.

But then, it doesn't seem that any of this will matter in a few short days. It's Wednesday, so if Tommy and Joe want to get us out of here by the end of the weekend, that means we'll only be in town for a few short days.

There are still several things I still want to do, but most of all, I want to get a hold of Nikki.

I'll text my brothers when I have a minute, but right now I'm going to text the person who's at the front of my mind.

Nikki.

CHAPTER TWENTY

T anner

I SIT, drumming my fingertips on the table, watching the rain splatter against the window. I've just gotten off the phone with James, and the decision has all but been made. We're leaving town as soon as possible.

I hoped the delay with the bus would be long enough for us to stay in town for a few more days, but I know that James and Tommy are right. We have to get going, or the fans will be pissed off.

I briefly think about the fact that I have the tattoo shop to fall back on, but if I drop out of the band to be with my family, I'm going to have to figure out a way to move the business out here. I can't see Caitlyn wanting to move away from her hometown, or Arya wanting to get out of here when all her friends are here.

Sure, I don't have a problem leaving everything I've ever

known behind, but I can't ask that of my family. That is, assuming we're going to actually be a family.

My phone chimes and I glance down. I don't know who I am expecting, but my heart leaps into my throat when I see it's Caitlyn. It's the first I've heard from her since blowing her off the day before, and I'm not sure how I'm going to tell her that I might have to leave again so soon.

I want to tell her that I want to consider doing something long distance while I'm away, but I can't find the words to do it. I haven't even found the words to tell her that I've been thinking about her, period. Reluctantly, I open the message.

If you're not too busy, your daughter wants to see you today. She's not happy about you leaving her hanging yesterday. Her mother is even less happy about it.

I cringe. I don't want to fight with Caitlyn, but I know next time I see her I'm going to get an earful about how I didn't come see them when I could. I don't know how to reply, so I keep it short and to the point.

Great, I would love to see you guys.

I hit send before I have the chance to change my mind, and I'm surprised when my phone immediately starts ringing. Part of me is relieved that it's Nikki, and not Caitlyn, calling me.

"Hello?"

"What're you up to?" Nikki sounds cheerful enough, a welcome change from the disappointment of my ex.

"Not much. Trying to figure out another time to see Arya before I go. I guess we're going to be leaving soon." I don't know how much she knows, and I honestly don't give a fuck. I feel tense enough about the situation with my daughter, and I don't have the time to tiptoe around how she's feeling as well.

"You are? That's too bad. I was wondering if you wanted to do something this afternoon?" If I didn't know better, I'd think she sounded jealous. But I thought we'd cleared that up the other night and that she was happy being just friends.

"Well, I just agreed to meet with my daughter. I hope you understand," I say after a moment of hesitation. The last thing I want is for both women to be mad at me, but I have to start prioritizing.

"Are you just hanging out with Arya?" Nikki asks at last. This time, I can tell by her voice that she's fishing for information, and I sigh. I don't want to have this conversation with her, and I hope we aren't going to end up having a fight. At the same time, I have to stick to how I'm feeling. And besides, we seemed to be on the same page since hanging out the other night.

"I don't know. I want to make things work with Caitlyn, but I know she thinks I'm going to hurt her again. I don't know what to do." I don't know how or why I feel so comfortable opening up to Nikki, but I know I can trust whatever she has to say.

"Do you know what I think?" she asks at last. I hesitate a moment, not sure if I really do or not.

"I'd love to know what you think," I lie.

"I think you should take them both out. See what it's like to hang out with the two of them, and see if you and Caitlyn can get along. She's hurt, Tanner, as I'm sure you are. But I think you both want to do what is best for your daughter, and I'm sure you've both thought about the idea of being a family. If there's still something between the two of you, you need to decide together if it's worth giving it another try." I can hear something of truth in her voice, and I leap on the opportunity.

"Do you know if she said something in therapy? Do you think I might have a shot at getting back together with her?" I ask eagerly.

"Therapists aren't allowed to divulge anything that is said during a therapy session, not even to other therapists," she replies, but I can hear in her voice she wants to say so much more.

"All right, then, I think I will take them out," I say at last.

"I think that's a great idea. Just don't push her. Be yourself, and see what happens. You two fell for each other the first time around by being open and honest, so do that again."

Her words give me more hope than I've felt in a long time. Never in my life have I wanted to kiss her so badly. But then, never in my life have I wanted to make things right with Caitlyn as badly as I do just now, either.

"Thanks for your advice," I say at last, and I hear her gulp before she replies.

"You know I'd do anything for you," she says after a few seconds.

"I really do owe you one," I say quietly.

"Good luck," she says sweetly.

"Thanks."

I hang up the phone and run to the bathroom, making sure I'm trimmed and looking presentable for the woman I'm trying to win back. When I get back to the bed, I pick up my phone with a grin, unable to hide the smile on my face.

I'm going to take Nikki's advice. I'm not going to push Caitlyn, but I'm going to be very open to hearing everything she has to say about what she thinks our future can hold.

After all, this is my chance to get my family back. I'm willing to put anything and everything on the line to make that happen.

CHAPTER TWENTY-ONE

Nikki

I PACE back and forth in my apartment, telling myself I have to accept the fact that there truly is no future between me and Tanner.

Every time I think that I've gotten it through my head, an agitated feeling swoops in, as if letting go of the idea of him is the wrong choice.

I know I did the right thing telling Tanner to go out with Caitlyn and see if he can make things work with her, but it doesn't come without a price, and I feel the jab in my heart.

I'm starting to think that this weird feeling of jealousy I haven't totally been able to shake has less to do with Tanner and more to do with me. Of all my exes, he's the only one I was ever able to see a real future with. If he's going to be sharing his future with someone else, where does that leave me?

I've always pictured myself with a husband and babies in my future, but in the years since Tanner and I broke up, I haven't truly felt that strongly about anyone. Now, seeing Tanner with his daughter, and thinking of the possibility of a reconciliation between him and Caitlyn, is making me question whether I'll ever have that future I always dreamed about.

Shaking my head to clear it of this self-pity, I suddenly have an idea. There's no point in sitting around my apartment feeling sorry for myself. If going out with Tanner is off the table tonight, well, then, I'll just have to find someone else to occupy my time.

I consider calling James to see what he's doing, but there's something holding me back. I thought my date with James would be fun and casual, but there was something incredibly intense about being with him. I don't want to try to work out my feelings for him in my own mind tonight. Tanner said that they were planning on leaving soon, and I don't want to get anymore attached to James—that's just a guarantee that I'll get hurt again.

I know that, at best, I can consider what I have going on with both James and his brother a "friends with benefits" arrangement, but I still don't want to think about what will happen when he leaves. As much as I try to tell myself that there's nothing between us—we didn't speak any words to each other about a future. Other than his cryptic words about being ready to compete, we didn't even speak about our feelings. Since then, he's hardly spoken to me other than through text, so I imagine those words had more to do with his male pride than they did with his feelings for me.

And yet, still, I know that James leaving is going to tear a tiny little hole in my heart that's going to hurt worse than when Tanner left. At least when Tanner left the first time, he was breaking the heart of another girl.

All he did to me was break off our friendship in an abrupt and rude way.

Making a decision for myself, I look down at my phone and debate whether I should text Tommy first and ask him if it's okay if I come over. I can't imagine he will be doing anything at the hotel that I won't be able to join in on, but at the same time, I don't want to create an uncomfortable situation.

Why don't you just show up and fuck him? You know that will make you feel better, plus there are no worries that you're going to fall for him like you might with James ... the thought runs through my mind and I smirk as I walk over to my closet, pulling it open and looking over my more revealing clothing choices.

I select something in the middle. Not too showy, not too conservative. Something that will show him that I'm there with a specific intent, but nothing that too obviously screams out that I'm looking to fuck. I tease my hair and put it in a ponytail before heading over to the hotel.

Part of me is glad I don't run into any of the other brothers while I'm on my way up to Tommy's room. It's surprisingly easy to find his room from the woman at the front desk, but she does inform me that there are several Bridges on the floor, and she hopes I find the right one.

I assure her that I know all of the brothers, but as I make my way up to his room, I silently pray that I don't run into anyone else.

I square my shoulders and knock on the door, smiling as it swings open. Tommy looks at me in surprise, eyeing me from head to toe with a hungry look on his face.

"Sorry I didn't call first, but I thought we could have some fun this afternoon," I say with a grin. I walk into the room and put my hands on his shoulders, stepping up and kissing him. Tommy starts kissing me back, but there's something in his touch that makes me hesitate. I can sense something is different, but I don't know what it is.

I try to nuzzle into his neck, but once again I realize there's something wrong. He's definitely hesitating, and it feels like he's just on the verge of pushing me away. I take a step back, adjusting my clothing that was slowly falling free, looking at him with wide eyes.

"Are you okay?" I ask. He smiles, looking me over with the same hungry look, but clearly fighting with himself.

"I don't know if this is a good idea," he says.

I feel my heart sink. A knot quickly forms in the pit of my stomach, and I feel the pain of rejection take over.

"What's wrong? Is it something I did?" I ask, a little too harshly.

"What the fuck are you so upset about? You're the one who showed up here unannounced. What the fuck did you think was going to happen?" Tommy is also speaking harshly, and I wonder what the fuck happened since the last time I saw him.

"You didn't seem to mind it the last time we were alone with each other!" I snap as I cross my arms.

He looks at me with raised eyebrows, and I can see the old asshole that I remember so clearly in his expression. I begin to wonder why I ever thought there might be something else between us.

"That was before all that shit went down. Come on, Nikki, you know my lifestyle. You know that there isn't ever going to be anything between us," he says flatly.

I look at him with hurt in my eyes. It's true, I do know all that. That's part of the reason I came here in the first place, but I don't like the way it feels when he says so. Just like with Tanner, I don't like the feeling of rejection.

And now I've been rejected twice in as many days.

"You know, I don't know what I expected. Maybe for you to change? Maybe for you to think about a single goddamn person besides yourself? You tell me what I thought, Tommy, since you seem to know so much about me!" I don't know where this is coming from, even as it's coming out of my mouth, but I'm not going to back down now.

I'm not going to lie; after the week I've had, it feels good to fight. Even if the target might be a little misdirected.

He looks at me for a moment then shakes his head with a smirk on his face.

"You women are all the same," he says with a laugh.

I feel outraged, but I'm not going to argue about this any longer. I don't have to stand here and listen to him belittle me. I want to slap him, but I'm not even going to give him the satisfaction of knowing how much his words affect me.

I stand still and silent for a moment, my hands draped around the back of my neck, my elbows reaching down and covering my breasts. Then I smirk and look up at him with the same arrogance in my eyes that he has in his.

"You know what? You're right, we are all the same. But so are you!" I don't wait for him to answer me, turning on my heel and walking over to the door. I put my hand on the knob and hesitate, turning to look at him for a brief moment.

"I hope you find what you're looking for, Tommy. And I hope you make things right with your father before it's too late." I see his face change, and I know I've said the one thing that will push him over the edge.

I open the door and storm through, yanking it closed behind me. I don't care if the thud of it brings out his other brothers. I don't care what anyone thinks of this. I hurry up the hall and step into the elevator, ignoring the tears that have sprung into my eyes.

"Fuck him! Fuck all of them!" I mutter as I slam my hand against the ground level button. The door closes and I drag my hand against my eyes just one time.

I will not cry over this man, no matter what he says or does. In fact, I'll take it a step even further.

I will not cry over any man.

CHAPTER TWENTY TWO

Tommy

THE RAINSTORM that settled in this morning has turned into a full-blown thunder storm. The dismal weather has me even more agitated than I was right after Nikki left.

I wish I had a drink in my hand. I know that there's some liquor in the mini fridge in the corner of the room, but that's not good enough. I don't want to get drunk; I want to be drunk right now. I try not to think about what just went down with Nikki, but that's all my mind can seem to focus on.

Women are so confusing. Half the time they tell me one thing while doing the opposite—how am I supposed to understand that shit when they send so many mixed signals? If she had only called and asked me if she could come over, I would have told her over the phone that I didn't think it was a good idea. Then we could've avoided that nasty argument that just took place.

I might have asked her if she had something else going on with James, or if she was getting attached to me. I might have just told her that I'm ready to move on and I was happy for the fun time that we had the other night.

But now she's pissed at me and I'm pissed at her. I'm not sure who is more in the wrong, and I hate feeling like I'm the bad guy. I can blame her for so many things, but then my conscience gets in the way and tells me that I shouldn't have fucked her in the first place.

I have some issues with impulse control. There are many things that I enjoy immensely at the time, but that I soon start to wonder whether they were worth all the trouble they bring later. The sex with Nikki was amazing, but now I'm feeling like it would have been better just to admire her from afar.

Especially after the way James was questioning me about her.

I didn't want to hurt her feelings, but her showing up unannounced had me feeling a little panicked. I don't want her growing attached to me—especially if James is interested in her—and I don't want to be the person she goes to when she's not sure what she wants in life. Sure, it was difficult for me to turn down having sex with her, but I could tell something was off with her from the moment she walked into the room.

It was clear from the expression on her face—and the way she snapped at me—that something was eating at her, and I can imagine it must have had something to do with James.

I still don't have the full story from James over how he feels about her, but I do know that the two of them went out together. I suspect that, since he didn't elaborate on anything they did, that he must have some sort of attachment to her.

Not to mention the fact that he said he wasn't in too big of a hurry to get out of town. I'm not stupid; I know there's something going on, but I don't much care to figure out what it is.

They can all either tell me straight what's happening, or they can count me out of it.

My phone rings and I cuss under my breath, recognizing the number from the clinic.

"Hello?"

"Mr. Bridges?" I know it's the receptionist.

"Yes, what do you want?" I snap. I don't give a fuck about being professional with any of them anymore.

"This is Stef—" she begins, but I interrupt her.

"I'm in a hurry and don't have time for introductions. Can you just tell me what you want?" I snap once more.

"Sir, I am going to have to ask you to watch your tone. I'm calling on behalf of your father. He wants to speak with you, and he told me this is the only way to get a hold of you." Her voice is tart and to the point, and I roll my eyes.

"Look, lady, I don't care what my father wants. You can tell him that I tried, and he was nothing but the arrogant asshole that he's always been. He had his chance, and that's all he gets. Now, if you'll excuse me, I have a real life to get back to." I'm about to hang up the phone when she stops me.

"I understand your frustration, sir, but with the way the cancer is progressing, you should weigh your decisions carefully. You might not get another chance to see him if—"

I cut her off once more. "Lady, listen, I know how cancer works. Quite frankly, my relationship with my father is none of your business. Now, if you don't leave me alone, I'll report both the clinic and my father for harassment. Do I make myself clear?" I wait, too angry to feel like an asshole for the way I'm treating her.

There's a moment of silence before she hangs up the phone, not bothering to answer my question. I listen to the dial tone for a moment before throwing the phone across the room, letting it bounce off the wall and clatter to the floor.

I don't care if it breaks. I don't care if anyone can reach me or not. I don't even care about the band at the moment. Right now, all I want to do is vanish. I want the entire world to fuck off, and I want all the emotions that have washed over me this past week to just go away.

I sit with my head in my hands for a few moments, wondering if I should drown my sorrows in the rest of the bottle of whiskey that's in the mini fridge, or if I would be better off just leaving. I don't want to be like my father, and I worry the more I turn to whiskey to fix my problems, the more I become like him.

There are days when I don't give a fuck and drain it anyway, then there are days when I feel stronger than the man he was, and I stay away. Today, I don't want to be like him. Today I want to be so different from him that we aren't even recognizable as father and son.

Another idea comes to mind. I'm not going to stay here and deal with this shit. I'm not going to let life fuck me over anymore. I am going to take control, and I'm going to move on from all of this pointless drama.

If I have to fuck off and take care of myself for a few days, so be it. I'm going to get out of here, and I'm going to forget about this entire week. I can get my shit together in the next stop, and by the time the rest of the band pull their heads out of their asses and follow me, I'll be ready to put on the next show.

I find my phone and begin searching for flights out of town. I'll message James my plan when I get all the details worked out, and he can deal with the rest of the band. All I care about is getting out of town as soon as possible, and putting all of this behind me.

CHAPTER TWENTY-THREE

James

Why won't you answer your phone? What's wrong?

I hit send and wait impatiently. I've been trying to get a hold of Nikki all day, but she keeps sending me to voicemail. Normally, I would think she was at work, but the way the phone keeps ringing twice before going to voicemail leaves me thinking that she's avoiding me.

She answered a couple of my messages earlier in the day, but she's acting distant now, and I want to know what's wrong. I can't help but feel worried about her, especially since I know we'll be leaving in the next few days.

It's something I want to talk to her about, but I don't know when I'm going to get the chance. Finally, my phone chirps and I pick it up off the table, scanning the message and hoping to get a straight answer out of her.

I'm sorry, James, I'm just not feeling that great today. Can we talk another time?

I read the message a few times, shaking my head. What the fuck does she mean she wants to talk another time? Doesn't she know that I'm leaving? Sure, she might not know the exact plan, but she has to know that it's not going to be very long before I'm gone.

Besides that, I have to assume that she's heard from one of my brothers about exactly when we're leaving. She must know. But I can't just ignore this. I have to find out what's wrong with her.

I don't know if we're going to have another time. Can we please talk?

I wait a few more minutes, and when I don't get an answer, I try again to call her. The phone rings a few times, but then it's sent to voicemail again. I hang up, cussing under my breath. I hate it when women do this, and I hate it even more knowing it's Nikki acting like this.

Finally, I decide I'm sick of sitting around and waiting for her to answer the phone. I'm going to do what I think she would do if the situation were reversed. I'm going to put on a clean shirt and some cologne, and then I'm going to go over to her apartment.

If she's going to avoid me through the phone, then I'm going to show up and speak with her face to face.

It's really as simple as that.

"James! What are you doing here?" Nikki looks at me in surprise when she opens her door, and she quickly tries to close it in my face. I put my foot in the way.

"I'm worried about you, Nikki. Come on, please talk to me!" I plead. She hesitates, and I can see she feels torn. She debates for a moment, biting her lip as she thinks it over, then she opens the door.

"There really isn't a lot to talk about," she says simply.

I look at her. "Come on, you aren't acting like yourself. What happened?" I ask.

I look at her outfit. She looks like she went out. She's not dressed as she normally does, and I wonder if she was supposed to be meeting someone else. I remind myself that it's not any of my business, but I do feel a tingle of jealousy as I wait for her to reply.

"It's nothing, really. I just don't feel like talking." She turns to walk away from me when I suddenly have a hunch.

"Were you the one I heard fighting with Tommy earlier?" I ask. I cross my arms and raise my eyebrows, and she stops suddenly.

She turns slightly, looking over her shoulder at me. Her expression gives her away before she speaks, and I feel a knot in the pit of my stomach.

"How do you know about that?" she asks.

I smirk, not unkindly. "Honey, I'm pretty sure the entire hotel heard you leaving."

My words hang in the air for a few moments, and she looks away. I can see tears in her eyes, and I feel my stomach tighten. I don't want to think about what she might have going on with my brother, but I can't help it.

"Do you love him?" I ask. She looks at me with wide eyes.

"I love all of you. You know that. I always have," she says quietly.

I laugh, but it doesn't come out right. I'm not going to let her get off the hook that easily. "You know what I mean. Did he tell you that we're leaving in a few days? Did you tell him that you want to be with him and he shut you down? What is it? Come on, I know there has to be something. What is it?" I don't want to admit the pain that I'm feeling, and I'm fighting to keep my cool.

I remind myself that she and I never talked about doing anything more with each other, and I know that in her mind what we did was purely for fun. It's not her fault that I grew attached or that I want more. She is free to do as she pleases.

Besides, she told me she had been seeing someone else. Hell, I even had a hunch from the beginning that it was Tommy. But still, the reality of knowing that she would choose my brother over me kills me. And it makes me want to kill him to think that he would break her heart like this.

"No! I didn't. That's not what happened." She pauses for a minute, looking at the ground and biting her lip again. She's always done that when she's uncertain. "It was stupid, really. I mean, I feel bad about something I said about your dad, and I want to make it right. But then, he was mean about some things, too. I don't know. I know this isn't the kind of stuff you want to hear." She stops, and I shake my head.

Looking down at her outfit once more, I look into her eyes.

"Did you fuck him?" I ask. I know I don't want to know the answer, but I have to ask anyway. She looks like she was out to get laid, and I don't want to think that she chose to go to him for that, rather than me. I can see the pain in her eyes, and I'm afraid that's the only answer I need.

"All we did was fight," she says at last. I wonder about her hesitation, and then I glance down at her outfit once more.

"That's quite the outfit you're wearing—not what I'd expect from someone who's planning on picking a fight with someone," I remark.

She looks down at her outfit and crosses her arms over her chest, but it doesn't do anything to cover her cleavage. "I don't tend to pick my outfits based on who I might argue with that day," she snaps.

I smirk. "That's my point exactly." My words hang in the air for a moment, and then she shakes her head.

"Don't be that way, James. It ... doesn't help anything."

I feel anger rising in my chest, but I don't want to fight with her. I don't want to be the asshole that my brother was. She might have hurt him, too, but I'm going to show her that we aren't all the same.

"Well, I stopped by to make sure you're okay, and I'm glad to see you are. Get a hold of me if you need anything." I can see she's surprised, but she only nods, biting her lip once more, and I turn to go.

There are still many questions in my mind that I want answered, but I don't know how to ask them without sounding like I'm accusing her, or like I'm mad at her. More than anything, I just want her honesty. I never thought that would be hard to get from her.

I get back to the car and check my phone. There's a text from Tommy, and I cringe. He's the last person I want to hear from right now, but if he's texting me, he must have something important to say.

I'm over this shit town. I'm heading out on the next flight to New York. Get your shit together and tell everyone else to hurry up; we've got a job to get back to.

I read through the text several times, unsure of how to respond. If he's leaving as soon as possible, he could be gone as soon as the next day. That's a lot sooner than planned, and I wonder if Nikki knows. I glance up at her apartment window, briefly debating whether I should go back and tell her that Tommy's leaving.

After a few moments, I sigh and put my phone back in my

pocket. This is one thing I'm not going to get involved in. If she wants to know where Tommy was, she can get a hold of him herself.

As far as I'm concerned, she has my number, and if she cares, she can text me.

CHAPTER TWENTY-FOUR

Tanner

"I just wanted you to know that we had a really good time today," Caitlyn is looking at me with the same sparkling eyes I so fondly remember from years ago. I brush the hair out of her eyes, and it's an effort to resist the urge to kiss her.

"I'm glad. I think Arya enjoyed it." Arya is sleeping in the back seat of the car, and I wish I didn't have to say goodbye to her—to either of them.

"You said you were leaving again soon?" Caitlyn asks, and I nod.

"We've got to keep the tour going or we're going to run into issues with the label. They get pissed when we don't bring in enough revenue, or the fans get pissy because we have to cancel shows and shit." I look out the opposite window, expecting her to get upset with me.

"I get it. I guess I never understood that your life could be so demanding before, but I get it," she replies.

I turn back to her in surprise. "You do?" I raise my eyebrows and she laughs.

"Of course I do. I never minded that you were on the road a lot, Tanner. I never did. I just hated the fact you left me hanging like that." She looks over her shoulder at Arya. "I don't think you could do that to her again."

"I couldn't. I couldn't do it to either one of you again," I say. I want to ask her if she'll give me a second chance to prove that to her, but I bite my tongue. I don't know how to ask her, but I can sense she's waiting.

"Anyway, I hope you're going to keep in touch better," she says as she sits up. I can tell she's getting ready to get out of the car, and I assure her that I'm going to.

"You both are going to be hearing from me a lot," I say with a smile. There's a look of disappointed sadness in her eyes as she nods.

"I'll do a better job of keeping you up to date on what Arya is doing, too." She walks to the back of the car and opens the door, gently shaking our little girl awake.

"Come on, darling, it's time for us to go inside now," she says. Arya rubs her eyes sleepily.

"Is Daddy coming?" she asks. I feel a pang in my heart, and I wish I was.

"Not tonight. But you're going to get to spend a lot more time with him from now on," Caitlyn says with a smile. Arya looks sad, but she doesn't argue this time.

"Go inside now and get your pajamas on. I'm going to say goodbye to your Daddy then I'll be inside too." She lifts Arya toward the front seat, and I give her a kiss and a hug good night, wishing with all my heart that I didn't have to leave. Arya runs toward the house, as happy as can be, but each step she takes away from me is crushing.

Caitlyn comes back to the front and bends over. "Thanks again."

"You know, I would love to hear about what you're up to from now on too," I say with a smile. She gives me a weak smile in return, and I can imagine this is as difficult for her as it is for me.

"I'll do that," she says. I get the impression she wants to kiss me, but there's something holding her back.

She stands up and closes the door, giving me a light wave of her hand to send me off.

I reluctantly hit the gas, driving away, but the entire time I stare in the rearview mirror, wishing she stayed to watch me go.

I don't know what compels me to drive to Nikki's house, but I'm in front of her building before I can think to do anything else.

For some reason, she seems to be the only person I can talk to about this, and I need her advice. Perhaps it's because she's a therapist—she's obviously good at this kind of thing. Perhaps it's simply because we have a history together.

Whatever the reason may be, I feel as though she's the only one I can turn to in this situation, and I want to hear her advice.

"Tanner?" She looks at me in surprise when she opens her door.

"Hey. I was wondering if you wanted to go grab a drink," I say nervously. She looks me over from head to toe, and I can see the confusion in her face. I don't want her to get the wrong impression, so I quickly add, "I just got back from hanging out with Caitlyn and Arya. I really need to talk."

There's a bit of hesitation on her face, but this time, I don't think it's jealousy. I'm asking her for help as a friend, and she knows that.

"But it's like eleven at night," she says, looking over her shoulder.

"I know it's late, but seriously, you are the only one I know who will give me the advice I need here." I laugh nervously, hoping that she can see the humor. I also notice that she's dressed as though she's just gone out, or perhaps is about to go out.

"Do you have plans?" I ask. She looks down at her outfit, evidently embarrassed by the tight T-shirt and the low-slung jeans. She might look professional when she's at work, but she also knows how to dress down. I have to admit she looks incredible.

"Oh no. I met up with a friend earlier, and I haven't had the chance to get into anything comfortable yet. Okay, if you feel like you really need to talk about this now then let's go." She reaches behind the door and grabs her jacket, slipping it around her shoulders as we make our way back down to my car.

I can feel my heart pounding in my chest, but not because I'm nervous around Nikki. I'm more nervous about the advice she's going to give me—nervous that she's going to tell me that this is all a bad idea, or that I'm making a mistake by wanting to take this risk that might mess with my daughter's life.

But I'm tired of running from my feelings. I'm tired of not being sure of what I want, or being too afraid to act on what I think I want to see if it's going to work out. I know Nikki can help me work this out in my head.

We drive down to the nearest bar and take a seat inside, and I'm glad there aren't many people in there. She orders a drink and sits down opposite me, looking at me with raised eyebrows.

"So, what's so important that you had to come get me at eleven at night to talk about it?" she asks. She's holding her glass with both hands, and I can see she's preparing herself for a long conversation. I settle in with my own beer, taking a few deep breaths before I begin.

"I want you to give me your honest opinion here. Don't just tell me what you think I want to hear," I begin.

She looks at me with a laugh. "Since when have I ever told you what you want to hear?" she asks.

I shrug. She does have a point with that one. When she and I were dating, that was one of the issues we had. I always thought her rather brutally honest, and she never had a problem with me thinking so.

"All right, then, you'll give me the truth, so I'll tell you the full truth," I say with a grin. I take a long swig of my beer before I begin.

"So it's about me and Caitlyn ..."

CHAPTER TWENTY-FIVE

Nikki

I DO my best to shut out the world, only focusing on what Tanner is saying. Once we sit down, I figure he'll have a lot to say, so I settle in and prepare myself for a long speech. As it turns out, I am right.

As we sit together, he starts at the beginning—of his relationship with Caitlyn. I suspected that he was going to want to talk about her, but he starts to bring up things that I had no idea about. He tells me how he felt about her while they were together. He tells me how he felt when he left her. He even tells me how he felt when he found out that they had a child together.

I always assumed he was angry with her, thinking that she got pregnant on purpose to trap him into a relationship. But from the way he describes it to me now, I believe he really was happy to learn that Arya was his, and is glad too that Caitlyn is her mother.

The more he goes on about how he feels about Caitlyn, the more I can see that he and I will never work out. I can see even more clearly why he and I didn't work out in the first place, and it helps free me of any lingering feelings of regret. Closure can really do wonders for a person.

By the time he finishes, I don't have much to add, but he waits for me to say something.

"Well, what do you think?" he prompts.

"What do I think about what, Tanner? You've told me on numerous occasions that you are still in love with this girl. You come to me and tell me that you want to make things work with her, and you tell me that you think she's the one. But whenever you're with her, you fucking don't do anything and just let her go." I take a long swig of my own drink, trying to tamp down my annoyance. Can't any of these men just be honest with the women in their lives?

He looks at me with a hurt expression. "Wow, I know you're a therapist and all, but I didn't think you were going to be so abrupt. Aren't you supposed to help people with their problems?" He looks down at his beer, and for a moment I feel sorry for snapping at him. But the feeling is short lived.

"You're the one who says that you want to be with her, but then you keep coming to me with all your feelings. Don't you think if you really want to be with her, you should be telling her all this?" Again, I don't mean to be so rude to him, but I've already dealt with too many men tonight not telling the women they're involved with how they feel.

We sit in silence for a few moments and he takes another drink of his beer.

"So how did your date go?" he asks, changing the subject.

I look at him in surprise. "What do you mean?"

"You said you were meeting with a friend earlier, and you look fantastic. I assumed that meant you had a date." There's a bit of a pause as I look down at my outfit, wondering for the hundredth time that day why I decided to put on something so revealing.

"It wasn't a date. I was going to meet with one of your brothers, but it didn't exactly go as planned." I take another drink, but nearly cough when he speaks again.

"James?"

"And why would you assume it's James?" I snap. I catch myself, suddenly realizing my own reaction gives me away. He looks at me and says nothing, finishing his beer.

I sigh. "I wanted to talk to Tommy about your father and ... some other things. But it didn't go well. Then I tried to talk to James, but I was so high-strung after the tension with Tommy that that didn't go well, either. Now I bet they both hate me." I finish my own drink and he laughs.

"First of all, I don't think there's anything you could do that would make either of them hate you—we've known you too long for that. Second of all, can't you see how badly James wants to be with you? The fuck are you doing? If you want to settle down with someone, why are you being so fucking blind?" He shakes his head and orders another beer, and I look at him with shock in my eyes.

I know that's the topic I've been avoiding in my own life for the past week, but I didn't know it was so obvious that someone like Tanner could see right through what I've been doing.

"I don't know what you're talking about," I say defensively.

He laughs. "Okay, you can keep telling yourself that. But if you recall, I've always been good at knowing when you're lying to me." He pops the cap off his drink and the bartender puts another glass in front of me.

"I don't know what you're talking about, and I wish you

would get off your high horse and come back to the rest of society," I say sarcastically. He's drinking his beer quickly, and I know he's trying to bring an end to the night, and his feelings.

"You can tell yourself whatever it is that makes you sleep at night, but you and I did date—not to mention all the years we were friends before that—and I know you better than you would like to admit." Tanner finishes his beer then nods toward my drink. "Are you going to stare at that all night, or are you going to finish it?"

I drink it quickly, trying to find some dignity in this conversation. He asked me out for advice, but now I feel like I'm the one who needs the therapy session. But I'm not going to give him the satisfaction of thinking that he is the one who helped me.

"I've changed a lot since back then, you know," I say after I finish the drink.

He chuckles and shakes his head. "You know what they say: the more things change, the more they stay the same. You, my dear, may have changed a lot, but for every little thing that has changed about you, there are a hundred things that have stayed the same." He lifts his hand and the bartender brings the tab. He pulls out his wallet and pays, but I sit, dumbfounded.

For the first time since he's gotten back, Tanner has rendered me completely speechless. We walk back to the car and he gets in, but I'm still stunned by the way the conversation has gone.

I'm a little surprised that he still knows me so well, even after all these years. Maybe he does have a point. And maybe that means James knows me just as well, too.

We make small talk on the way back to my house, but he drops me off once more outside my apartment.

"Are you sure you're not going to be too lonely tonight? You're not back with Caitlyn yet," I say, only half teasing. Sure, I might be over the idea of us getting back together, but I've always had a tendency to make bad decisions when I'm feeling out of control emotionally. And he does look very good tonight.

He laughs as he looks at me. "You say that now, but I bet you'll feel differently when the drinks wear off in the morning." I try to argue with him, but he drives away, leaving me standing in the street, wishing he'd come up.

After the day I've had, I don't want to spend the night alone. But I know he made the right decision—for both of us.

I remain outside in the dark for a few moments, trying to ignore the thoughts about James that my conversation with Tanner brought up. I know now that my feelings are anything but casual for him, and a part of me thinks it would still be easier if I just had them for Tanner instead. After all, it's safe to dream about Tanner. I can think that there's a chance for the two of us, with the assurance that it's never again going to happen.

With James, I'm scared. I know that he could be mine, and I know that he could break my heart. It's thrilling and terrifying all at the same time, and as much as I want it, I know that I'm not ready to reach out and grab it yet.

I go upstairs and slip out of my jeans and my bra, leaving only the tight T-shirt and panties on. I collapse into bed, telling myself that it's Tanner I wish was in my bed. I'm not scared to act on my feelings. I just have to direct them toward the one that I know isn't going to love me back.

I know it's stupid, and I know it's not going to work, but I also know it's safe.

It's safer to not fall in love.

CHAPTER TWENTY-SIX

Tommy

I PULL up in front of Nikki's apartment, unsure of what I'm going to say or how I'm going to say it. All I know is that I treated her badly yesterday, and I can't leave things like that between us.

There is a part of me that knows I was right to turn her down yesterday. She and I would never work, and I need to move on. But there's another part of me that wonders what it might be like—and what the hell have I got to lose anyway? If she feels like giving it a shot, then why the fuck not? But if I want to figure out what Nikki's feeling, then I'm going to have to get over that and see what I can do.

I got a hold of her as soon as I could that morning and managed to convince her to let me drop by for coffee. Now that I'm in front of her apartment, I pause and think about what I'm going to say. As always, the best thing to do seems to be to just get in and tell her straight what I'm thinking.

"Hey," she says when she opens the door. She's wearing the same T-shirt from yesterday, but I can tell she's not wearing a bra underneath. She's also slipped into pajama shorts. Seductive, but she's not acting like it's intentional.

She lets me in and we settle down at her kitchen table with our coffee.

"Well, first of all, I want to say I'm sorry for the way I spoke to you yesterday. Being back here has really messed with me, and I know I treated you unfairly." She nods her acceptance of my apology, and I take a deep breath, bracing myself for the rest of the conversation. "I don't think there's really an easy way to say this, so I'm just going to say it," I say after taking an awkward sip of my coffee.

"Go ahead," she prompts.

"Do you want to give a relationship a shot? I mean, I thought about what happened yesterday, and I don't know. Maybe you and I would be good together. Who knows?" I'm about to continue, but she holds up her hand.

"Tommy, I know how you're feeling, but I think it's just nostalgia. I think you're more upset about what happened with your father than about what happened with me, and I think you're turning to me to fix it. You're looking to form a stable relationship now that your relationship with your father is so unstable. But you don't really want to be with me, and honestly, I have feelings for someone else." She smiles at me, and I feel a pang run through my chest.

But then another feeling runs through me—a feeling of peace. I suddenly realize she's right. This whole visit, I've been looking to her to fix my feelings about my father. And that isn't fair to her.

But I also can't help but wonder who she has feelings for—though there's a part of me that already knows.

"James?" I ask.

She nods. "I know I should have told you before, but I didn't want to make it awkward. I'm sorry, Tommy." She's speaking quickly, but I stop her.

"I'm not mad about it. I'm glad you told me now, and you never told me you weren't seeing someone else. It makes it somewhat awkward, but less." We both laugh, and I see her with newfound respect.

"I don't know if you've heard, but I'm going to be leaving this afternoon. I'm sick of this town and all that it's done to me. I'm glad you and I were able to reconnect, and thanks for trying with me and my dad, but I think it's time to move on." I drain the rest of my coffee and get up to go. She sets her cup down too, also getting up.

She puts her hand on my shoulder, looking into my eyes with the same searching look she always has. There's something about the way she gazes at me that makes me feel like she can see into my soul. Talking to her is like talking to someone who really and truly cares, and I hope that our awkward romantic interlude won't ruin that in the future.

"I know you didn't come to me for advice, but I'm going to give it to you anyway," she says with a grin. "I think you should go see your father."

The words sting, and I give her a look that tells her exactly how I feel. Before I have the chance to argue, however, she lifts her finger.

"Just hear me out. Your father is going to pass away one day, and you are never going to get the chance to speak with him again. I know it's hard now, but you'll be glad that you took the time to at least tell him goodbye. Trust me, I know what it's like to have a difficult dad, but I'm telling you, this is for you, not for him." She's still looking into my eyes as she speaks, and I feel the urge to kiss her.

I want to take her in my arms and take out all the frustration

I'm feeling on her. I want to feel what it's like to have sex with her once more, but I want her to look at me with that deep sense of caring. I want to feel that passion. But I know that's just avoiding the problem, and I know she can't give me what I need. She's not the one for me, and I can't keep turning to her to fix my problems.

The time will come when I have to face how I feel about my father, and if what she's saying is true, I should do that today, rather than later.

"So what do you think I should do? Show up and just tell him that I'm leaving?" I ask with a sneer at the very idea. I can't imagine that will go any better than the last visit.

But she's undeterred. With a shrug, she picks up her coffee once more. "I don't care what you say to him. All I'm saying is that you should stop by and tell him that you're leaving, and that you wanted to see him one more time before you go. Trust me, it'll mean the world to both of you." She takes a drink of her coffee, and for a brief moment, all I can see is her glorious body and the bottom of her coffee mug.

She finishes it and sets it on the table with a clink, then she puts her hands on her hips and looks at me.

"You are obviously free to do what you please in this situation, but I'm telling you what I would do. Trust me, I've spoken to many people who let their relationship with a parent go unresolved before their death, and I know how difficult it can be to recover from that. It's my job as your friend to make sure you do the right thing while you can." She smiles up at me and puts her hand on my shoulder once more.

On a sudden impulse, I pull her close, hugging her tightly. There's nothing sexual about the moment, just the relief of me finally letting go of some of the anger I've been holding on to for so long. She hugs me tightly in return before pulling back and looking up into my eyes.

"Try to keep in better contact with me?" she asks.

I grab my phone off the table and slip it into my pocket, heading for the door. "I'll do my best. If I don't text you, text me."

She promises she will, and I glance back at her as I close the door behind me. I walk down to my car, thinking that I'll just going to head to the airport and wait for my flight.

But as I drive through town, I can't help but think about what she said. I know she's right. I'm going to have to face the fact that my dad is going to die—and soon. I can either do that now, or I can wait until it's too late.

I doubt that I will regret just leaving without seeing him again, but there's a small voice in the back of my mind that whispers that I might.

Perhaps it's a bad idea, and perhaps this is the one thing that I'm going to regret most in my life, but for once, I'm going to take her advice. At the last second, I take the turn to the clinic. I'm not sure what I'm going to say to my father when I get there, but I hope that it's going to go better than last time.

But no matter what happens with Dad, I know I'm going to get on the plane this afternoon with the satisfaction of knowing that I went through with it. I can live out the rest of my life knowing that I at least tried to make things right with my father.

Nikki seems to think it's just what I need to find peace, and I'm going to take her word for it.

CHAPTER TWENTY-SEVEN

James

I KEEP my eyes on the pavement in front of me as I walk, pretending that I don't notice the people I'm passing on the street. I can feel the glances in my direction when I push past those with children or dogs, but I'm not interested in being friendly, or even polite for that matter.

Tommy called me about an hour ago, telling me that he was about to get on his flight to New York City. There's a part of me that's upset that he's gone. It's bringing about a finality that I really do have to move on. I know that I'm going to be flying out of town in the next couple days, and I want to speak to Nikki again before I do, but the fact that Tommy is already gone is putting the pressure on.

I was surprised to hear that he decided to stop by and say goodbye to Dad before he left. I don't know what convinced him to do that, but he sounded glad that he had. He told me that it went better than the other day, and Dad told him he was happy to see us all again. I assured Tommy I would take the time to say goodbye before I left as well, though, right now, Nikki is really the only one I want to see.

I haven't really talked to her since I stopped by the other night. I want to text her, but I don't like the feeling I get when she brushes me off or ignores me—something she's been doing a lot lately. I don't know what the fuck is wrong with her, and it angers me that she isn't being upfront with me.

Up until our argument the other night, I was having such a fantastic time getting to know her again—not just on our date but through our text messages. And I thought that she was enjoying it too. I know that she couldn't have faked the connection I felt when we had sex.

I wish I knew what was going on inside her head, but I don't have anyone to talk to about it.

Tommy returned the rental car that morning, so I decide to take myself for a walk around town. I tell myself it's just a coincidence that I end up just around the corner from Nikki's apartment. I justify it to myself, telling myself that I don't have any idea if she's home or not.

How could I? I haven't messaged her or called her, and she hasn't made any effort to keep in contact with me, either. I tell myself that this is perfectly normal, though I find it harder and harder to resist the urge to go up and see her when I walk by.

When I get outside her apartment building, I stand with my hands in my pockets, looking up at the window. I can't tell if she's home or not; the afternoon sun is glistening off the window too brightly for me to see anything inside. But it looks like most of the cars are in their spaces, and I can't imagine she is working on a Saturday.

I pace back and forth in front of the building for a moment, and then I can't take it any longer. With a sudden impulse surging through me, I walk up to the door and head inside. There are a couple of tenants coming down the stairs, but they ignore me and I say nothing to them as I push my way past.

I hesitate once more when I reach her door, but once again my impulsiveness wins out and I knock loudly. I hear the sound of someone walking around inside, and my heartrate increases as she opens the door.

"James! How nice to see you," she says. I notice she glances in the hall, looking up and down both ways as though she's expecting someone. I also notice by her outfit that she looks like she's getting ready to go out. I try to ignore the surge of jealousy that runs through me.

I know Tommy is out of town now, so I have no idea who she could possibly be seeing now.

"Am I interrupting something?" I ask, looking at her with a smile. I try to mask my jealousy, but it only gets worse when she clearly evades of the question.

"I was just getting ready to go out. I didn't know you were planning on stopping by—you didn't bother to say anything." She makes a show of checking her phone, and I put my hand over it, gently pushing it down.

"I know. You don't bother to really answer me when I do try to get a hold of you, so I decided it was best to just show up and see what you were up to." I give her a look, and I can see her getting defensive.

"I didn't know that I had to answer you. After all, we haven't really talked about much besides sex the past few times we've been together."

I raise my eyebrows. I know she enjoys flirting as much as I do, and the fact of the matter is that we haven't discussed the fact that we had sex.

"Oh really? I was under the impression that you enjoyed

what we did the other night." I cross my arms and look at her, and she crosses her arms in defiance.

"I liked what we did well enough, but I'm not sure what it all means. Your brother seems to have the right idea, telling me how he really feels!" I can see by the look on her face that she doesn't mean to let those words slip out, but once they are out, it's too late.

"My brother? Tommy?" I snap. I know I have her in a corner now, and she has no choice but to tell the truth. "Do you have something going on with Tommy? I thought you said there was nothing going on there anymore."

The question is too direct for her to avoid, and she opens her mouth and closes it again. I can see she's grappling for an answer, but there isn't anything coming to mind.

"We slept together one time, but that was it," she replies with a flat tone after a moment of silence. "Then today he told me how he really feels about things."

I pause. I wonder exactly what he said. He told me that he didn't know how he felt about her, and he never really said anything else about it. At the same time, he didn't mention her at all when we spoke before he got on the plane. I wish I could ask her what she means, but she's angry and putting on her jacket, as if she's getting ready to just leave.

"So, since he's more open with me, I happen to know where we stand. If you'll excuse me, there are some things that I need to do." She's slipping on her shoes, but I'm not going to let her go just yet.

"What do you mean? Is there something you want to talk about?" I ask. I can see in her eyes that she has more she wants to say, but she's holding back. She pulls away from me and grabs her purse.

"I told you, James. When you want to be more open with me, then you can come talk to me. Until then, I'm not going to play these games with you!" She pushes past me and I follow, and she closes the door behind us.

"Where are you going?" I ask. She looks at me, her eyes on fire. I can see there's something wrong, but I can't guess what it is.

"I told you, I've got things to do!" she repeats. Before I have the chance to answer, she turns and walks up the hall, her shoes clicking on the floor. I stand in awestruck silence, shaking my head.

Tommy's right. Women are confusing.

CHAPTER TWENTY-EIGHT

Tanner

"Sorry, I got caught up with something at the last second." Nikki says breathlessly as she steps up to the bar. I can see right away she looks distracted, but my mind is too full of what I have going on to worry about what she's doing.

"I appreciate you coming to meet me at the last second anyway," I say. She looks at me with a smile, but it looks a little sad. She's also looking at me a little too speculatively, and that makes me nervous. I thought we'd sorted that all out, and I hope she's not thinking that I'm going to suggest that anything happen between us before I leave.

"No problem. You know I'll always be here for you, Tanner," she says with a smile. I clear my throat and look down at the glass in my hands.

"I was going to order you a drink, but I didn't know what you'd feel like so early in the afternoon," I say with an uncomfortable smile. She looks at me with a flirtatious grin, though she doesn't put much effort into it, and I look away once more.

"You know what I like. I would have been happy with anything, really. But since I'm ordering for myself, I'll take a vodka cranberry." She turns her attention to the bartender as he walks up, and after checking her ID, he goes to get her the drink. I wait patiently, trying to form my thoughts as she settles into her seat.

She looks at me patiently, leaning her cheek on her hand as she sits on her barstool.

"So, you're probably wondering why I asked you over here so suddenly," I say with a smile. She nods slightly, her hair bouncing as she does so.

I thought long and hard about what I was going to say, but now that she's sitting in front of me, I'm finding it difficult to tell her. I don't want to hurt her feelings, but I sense that I'm about to, especially with her in this weird mood.

"Well, I just wanted to tell you that I really owe you for this past week. I've been thinking a lot about what you said, and I think you're right. I have been coming to you when I really should have been going to Caitlyn, and I appreciate the way you've been listening to me all this time. I also realize that I've been unfair to you in doing so—all these unpaid therapy sessions," I give her a tiny grin, "but it's going to have to stop." I speak as gently as I can, but I can see her face change. There's something in her eyes, though she's still smiling.

It's silent for a moment, and the bartender awkwardly sets her drink down in front of her. She looks up at him and gives him a warm smile, and I can't help but wonder if she's doing it to avoid looking at me.

The silence is growing uncomfortable, but at last, she speaks.

"I am happy for you. I really am." I can hear her voice cracking, and she doesn't sound as convincing as she probably intended.

I'm starting to think there's really more going on here than what she's letting on. But I try to stick to us—if she wants to tell me something, she knows I'll listen.

"Hey, I'm not saying that we can't stay in contact, or that I'm going to stop talking to you again. I just wanted you to know that I've really thought about what you said, and I'm going to take your advice. But that doesn't mean we stop being friends. You know you can talk to me about anything, too." I smile, trying to draw her out a little.

I put my arm around her, and she sits silently for a moment. There are tears in her eyes, but she turns away and drags her hand across her face. I sit silently, giving her the moment to herself and wishing we had a conversation like this when I decided to leave town—maybe we wouldn't have lost so many years of friendship if I did.

After a few moments she turns back to me with a smile and takes a deep breath before sipping on her drink.

"Well, this doesn't have to be sad now, does it? Though I am going to miss you, you know" she says with a sly grin. I look at her in surprise, glad she's putting on a brave face in spite of whatever emotions she's feeling, but at the same time wondering why she doesn't seem in a rush to leave. I know that reconnecting with me and my brothers has brought a lot of confusion into her life, and I know a lot of that confusion centers around her feelings for me.

But if I'm going to be true to my word and be a real friend to her, then I'm going to have to stick around for these awkward times—and hopefully one day, they won't be so awkward anymore. I know it's going to be easier for me than it is for her, since I've got my future mapped out with Caitlyn.

To further my surprise, she starts to ask me about my plans.

"Are you guys going to be getting together quickly, or are you going to be taking it slow and seeing how it goes?" she asks, looking at me with wide eyes as she sips on her drink.

I sigh. "There's a lot I have to prove to her before she's going to trust me like she used to, but I know she will with time. It's not going to be easy, but I'm serious about this. I love her, and I'm going to make sure I'm the boyfriend and father that I should be. Maybe even someday I'll be a husband and father." I add the second part with a shrug, and she looks at me with surprise etched across her face.

"I never thought you were one for marriage," she says with a laugh. I shrug once more. The truth is I never thought I would find someone to settle down with, either, but at the same time, I never thought I would meet someone like Caitlyn again.

"I guess when you meet the one, you're willing to do things you never thought possible before," I say. She falls silent, and I suddenly realize we've only been talking about me.

"So, how are things going with you and James?" I ask. She looks at me with a bit of a glare, and I laugh. "Oh? It's going that well, is it?" I say sarcastically. "I thought you two had something going."

"Who told you that?" she asks, and I remember how testy she was being about it the other night, too. Maybe he's the reason for her weird mood today too.

"Don't you two talk? The way he talks about you, I would think that you two were dating by now." I sip on my drink and look at her, and I can see by the look in her eyes that she's feeling too many emotions to name. Surprise, flattery, sadness, confusion—just to name a few.

"I guess I could have been a little nicer to him this morning. I don't know. You would think being a therapist, I would be better at communication. But I guess it's one thing to give advice, and a whole other thing to trying to follow it." She shakes her head and I look at her with another inquisitive look on my face.

"What do you mean?" I ask.

"It's just that ... I don't know. I know that I like him. I mean I really like him. I'm just afraid. Who would have thought I would be the one who would be afraid to fall in love with someone?" She laughs, and I shake my head.

"Here you are, the person who's been telling me to go and pursue this woman I love in spite of the fact that it scares the shit outta me, and you're blowing off my brother when he's clearly head over heels in love with you?" I give her a teasing look, and she laughs once more. "What are you doing sitting here all sad at the bar with my sorry ass when you could be hanging out with him?"

"Well, I don't know if I would say that he's head over heels in love with me, but I do believe likes me." She smirks. "Though it's been a hell of a time trying to get him to admit that," she says with annoyance, and I laugh once more.

"Clearly you don't know him the way I do," I say. She suddenly appears agitated, and I look at my watch. "Is there somewhere you have to go?"

"I don't know. I just think I should go see what he's doing, maybe talk to him a little bit about all this, at least before he leaves town," she says.

I motion for the bartender to come over so I can pay the bill, then we head outside.

"Do you want a ride?" I ask, but she shakes her head. I can see the excitement in her face, and I pull her close. We hug, and for the first time since I've been back in town, I can't feel any lust in her touch. It's a pure embrace, and we enjoy the moment as friends.

"Thanks, Tanner," she says with a light squeeze, and I squeeze her back. She pulls back, looking at me with a smile, and I let her go. We say goodbye, and she turns and walks back up the block, but this time as she walks away I can see there's a skip in her step.

I put my hands in my pockets and turn away, ready to go find Caitlyn and see what she and Arya are doing. I'll stop by to see my father later this afternoon as well and tell him goodbye, making sure we end on a good note as well.

For the first time in my life, I feel that everything is coming together for me. For the first time in my life, I don't feel that there's anything in the world that can bring me down.

CHAPTER TWENTY-NINE

James

I DUMP everything out of my backpack and onto the floor, angrily shoving it from the floor and into the suitcase. I can't believe how badly things went with Nikki this morning, and I'm feeling frustrated that I still haven't told her how I feel about her.

I realize now that that's what she was wanting this morning, and I'm pissed that I missed such an easy opening. Why didn't I tell her this morning?

I want to tell her everything. I want to ask her to be my girlfriend, but the fact of the matter is that every time I'm around her, I feel my tongue tie, and I don't know how to say how I feel. I haven't tried to hide my feelings though, and I figure she must know but just doesn't feel the same.

Regardless of how she feels about me, I can't get her eyes out of my mind. I can't focus when I think about her. I've spent the last hour trying to think of our dad and how I'm going to handle things with him before I leave, but I can't keep those thoughts in my head for longer than a few minutes at a time.

Nathan called me earlier that afternoon and told me he and Janus already went over and talked to him, and I feel pissed off that they did it without me. It would have been far easier if we'd gone together. I could have gotten the goodbye out of the way without having to worry about how it would go with just him and me in the room.

But Tommy managed to go over and talk to him on his own, and from the sounds of things, it went just fine between the two of them. I want to believe that it will go the same for me, but then, thinking about how he and I rarely get along anyway, I don't have much hope.

My phone chimes and I glance down eagerly, hoping it's Nikki. I shake my head when I see it's Tanner, and don't even bother reading the message. I know he's going to tell me how well things are going for him and Caitlyn. While I'm happy for him, I'm also annoyed. Things always seem to work out for everyone else in the family but me, and I hate it.

I want to be able to tell everyone that I've found the love of my life, too, but the love of my life has already fucked one of my brothers and fallen for the other one. For all I know, she's out right now on some date with some other guy who's not even related to me.

She looked very nice this morning when she pushed past me in the hall, and I have no idea where she was going or who she was going to see. I find the entire situation more frustrating than I know how to deal with, and I can't wait to get out of town.

I can see why Tommy left the way he did, and part of me can't blame him. He's fine being a lone wolf, and I should be, too. I have my pick of the lot when it comes to getting laid. I should be happy that I don't have to deal with the commitment that comes with being in a relationship while on the road.

All these things continue to run through my mind, and it makes me even more impatient to get on a plane and get out of here. Suddenly, I hear someone knocking on the door, and I roll my eyes.

I don't want to deal with the maid right now, and I glance around, wondering if I remembered to put the Do Not Disturb sign on the door. I don't see it anywhere in the room, and I sigh. The knock comes again, and I throw my clothes on the floor.

"Fucking coming!" I snap as I head toward the door. There's another knock and I wonder how badly this maid wants to have her head ripped off. By the time I reach the door, I'm seething.

I yank open the door, ready to start yelling. But I stop short when I see who it is.

"Nikki? What are you doing here?" I ask in surprise. I glance up and down the hall, almost certain there has to be someone else with her. But she's clearly alone, standing in front of me with a smile on her face. I can see in her eyes that she's nervous, but she looks every bit as beautiful as she did when I saw her that morning.

Even more beautiful, actually, because she doesn't look pissed at me this time.

"I was wondering if I might come in for a few minutes?" she asks, looking at me with those same wide eyes I've spent the last few hours obsessing over.

"Are you sure you want to?" I ask, crossing my arms and looking down at her with raised eyebrows. If she's here for a fight, I would rather shut the door in her face than get into another screaming match with her.

"Do you have someone in there with you?" She frowns, trying to glance around me.

I smirk at her.

"Do I look like I might?" I ask flatly. I don't want her to suffer, but then, I don't want her to think that I'm too eager for her to come inside, either. As long as I have some power in this situation, I'll be happy.

"I don't know. I just want to talk to you for a minute. It's important." Her smile fades slightly, but it comes back quickly as she tries to regain her composure. I can see she's fighting to keep this confident façade up, but her eyes are betraying her. She's clearly very nervous, and I have to admit that I'm enjoying watching her squirm just a bit.

But with the way her lower lip is quivering, I can't put her through this very long.

"Okay, you can come in," I say at last, pushing the door open.

"I'll only be a minute," she says with a smile.

"Please, take your time," I say sarcastically, closing the door and looking at her with expectation in my face.

I fully expect her to start yelling, but she takes me by surprise.

CHAPTER THIRTY

Nikki

"Look, James, I understand if you hate me, but I had to get this off my chest. I'm so sorry for how I've been acting. I should have been more honest with you." I look at him with as sincere a look as I can, trying to fight off tears at the thought that he might not forgive me. He watches me for a moment in silence, his arms crossed.

"I need to know. Do you love Tommy?" he asks.

I shake my head. I can see by the way he's looking at me that this really bothers him. He wants to know the truth, and he's not going to be happy until he knows I've told him exactly how I feel.

The way his eyes are boring into mine, I feel as though he can see into my very soul. I know that I have no choice but to tell him the full truth, and for the first time, I'm not afraid to do so. I want him to know what happened, and I want him to know how I'm feeling now.

I don't want there to be anymore secrets between us. I want him to know anything and everything about me. For the first time in as long as I can remember, I'm willing to be entirely vulnerable with him. I'm willing to tell him the truth and hope for the best.

It's not going to be easy, but I'm willing to give it a try. If things work out, it will have been worth it.

"We slept together—before you and I even went out—but I told you, we talked about how we felt, and we're done. It wasn't anything serious. I don't love him as anything more than a friend, James. I don't." I shake my head and take a step forward.

"I'm so sorry for how I've been treating you. I know I don't deserve your friendship, but please, give me another chance. I don't want to lose you, I really don't. You're ... special to me." I put my hands on his shoulders, but before I'm able to continue, he leans forward and presses his lips to mine.

I'm surprised, but I don't pull away. I wrap my arm around his neck, pulling him toward me and kissing him with a growing passion. Our tongues dance around each other; I press my body against his, trying to get as close to him as I can.

I prepared so many things to say to him, but sometimes words aren't the most effective way of communicating. Words can wait.

He begins tearing my clothing off, and I'm quick to do the same. He throws me back on top of the bed, and within seconds he's on top of me, his tongue exploring every part of my body. I moan and writhe on the bed, allowing him to explore freely.

All at once he's on top of me, his hard dick pressed against the opening of my tight pussy. We're already breathing hard, our faces only inches apart, our eyes boring deeply into each other.

Without saying a word, he pushes himself inside me. I gasp

at the sensation, raising my hips to meet him, taking him as deeply as I can.

He pulls himself out and pushes himself into me again, drawing out his full length then filling me as full as he can. He's going faster and faster, and I am dragging my nails down his back, enjoying each second of him fucking me.

Our lips lock, our tongues intertwine. He's moaning and thrusting deeper and faster, and I'm no longer able to control myself. I raise my hips as I'm consumed by an orgasm, the waves of pleasure rocking my entire body.

At almost the same time, I see a twitch in his face and feel his cock pulse inside me. I feel him throbbing inside me. He leans down and groans sweet nonsense in my ears as his hips twitch against me.

When the sensation finally passes, we lie still, holding each other, and I feel him slowly growing softer inside me.

All too soon he rolls off me, falling naked on the bed. But I have no intention of leaving anytime soon. I crawl up and lay my head on his chest, enjoying the feeling of him running his fingers through my hair. I have never felt so satisfied in my entire life—both physically and emotionally—and for a brief moment, I wonder if this is what it would be like to be truly committed to someone.

I wonder what it would be like to know that this was the kind of sex I could enjoy all the time. Sure, I would have to share him with the rest of the world in public, but when we were in places like this, it would just be us.

We're silent for a few moments, and I can't help it any longer. I have to know what he's thinking. I have to tell him how I feel. But suddenly I don't know what to say. I don't know how else to apologize, and I don't know how to express how I'm feeling.

Even as a therapist, I feel frustrated, wanting to tell him so many things, but not able to find the words. I close my eyes and take a deep breath, for the first time in my life not worrying about saying the right thing, but only saying the thing that comes to my mind.

And the only thing that's on my mind right now is the sex we just had.

"As always, you're amazing," I say with a sigh, placing a gentle kiss on his pec. We're lying in his bed completely naked, and I look up into his eyes, running my hand over the scattering of hair on his chest. James looks down at me and puts his hand over mine, letting his other hand trail down my back.

"You know, we could do this all the time. I mean, as often as my schedule allows," he says with a laugh.

I look at him with raised eyebrows.

"How is that going to be possible, with how often you travel? I have a job here." I remind him.

He shrugs. "We can figure it out. All I know is that I love you, Nikki, and I don't ever want to let you go. You're by far the best thing that has ever happened to me, and I want this to continue for as long as we live. If Tanner can manage it with Caitlyn and Arya, I think you and I can manage." He looks into my eyes, and I feel my heart skip a beat.

He has never mentioned loving me before, and when I hear the words, I know that I feel the same way. I don't know when it happened, and I don't know how it happened, but I know without a shadow of a doubt that I do love him.

"I love you, too, James. You and only you. I think we can do this, too. We'll figure it out." I can see his face light up, and he shifts slightly to better look into my eyes.

"Do you mean it?" he asks, and I nod.

"I love you. From here on out, it's you and me," I say with a grin. He squeezes my hand and leans down, kissing me once more. I lay my head on his chest and let out a contented sigh.

I've never known what true love is before, but now that I've tasted it, I know I can never go back.

It might have taken some time for my brain to catch up with my heart, but I know that James is the one I've been waiting for. I love him more than anything, and I know this is going to work.

This is him and this is me.

From now on, this is us.

THE END.

SIGN UP TO RECEIVE FREE E-BOOKS AND AUDIOBOOK CODES.

Would you like to read **The Unexpected Nanny, Dirty Little Virgin** and **other romance books** for **free**?

You can sign up to receive these free e-books and audiobooks by typing this link into your browser:

https://www.steamyromance.info/free-books-and-audiobooks-hot-and-steamy/

Or this one:

https://www.steamyromance.info/the-unexpected-nanny-free/

OTHER BOOKS BY THIS AUTHOR

Other Books By This Author

Saving Her Rescuer: A Billionaire & A Virgin Romance

I was just trying to get away from my crazy ex for the weekend when I ended up in a giant pileup on the highway up to Gore Mountain.

https://geni.us/SavingHerRescuer

* * *

Sensual Sounds: A Rockstar Ménage

Lust. Lies. Double lives.

The rock and roll industry is full of people who are looking out for themselves and willing to do anything to rise to the top.

https://www.hotandsteamyromance.com/collections/frontpage/products/sensual-sounds-a-rockstar-menage

* * *

On the Run: A Secret Baby Romance

Murder. Lies. Fraud. Just another day in the lives of billionaires and women on the run.

https://www.hotandsteamyromance.com/collections/frontpage/products/on-the-run-a-secret-baby-romance

* * *

The Dirty Doctor's Touch: A Billionaire Doctor Romance

I am a master. An elitist. I am at the top of my field, and I know what I am doing.

https://www.hotandsteamyromance.com/collections/frontpage/products/the-dirty-doctor-s-touch-a-billionaire-doctor-romance

* * *

The Hero She Needs: A Single Daddy Next Door Romance

He's the only man I've ever wanted...

https://www.hotandsteamyromance.com/collections/frontpage/products/the-hero-she-needs-a-single-daddy-next-door-romance

* * *

You can find all of my books here

Hot and Steamy Romance

https://www.hotandsteamyromance.com

ABOUT THE AUTHOR

Mrs. Love writes about smart, sexy women and the hot alpha billionaires who love them. She has found her own happily ever after with her dream husband and adorable 4 year old. Currently, Michelle is hard at work on the next book in the series, and trying to stay off the Internet.
"Thank you for supporting an indie author. Anything you can do, whether it be writing a review, or even simply telling a fellow reader that you enjoyed this. Thanks

facebook.com/HotAndSteamyRomance

©Copyright 2020 by Michelle Love - All rights Reserved
In no way is it legal to reproduce, duplicate, or transmit any part of this document in either electronic means or in printed format. Recording of this publication is strictly prohibited and any storage of this document is not allowed unless with written permission from the publisher. All rights are reserved.
Respective authors own all copyrights not held by the publisher.

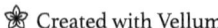 Created with Vellum

www.ingramcontent.com/pod-product-compliance
Lightning Source LLC
LaVergne TN
LVHW021720060526
838200LV00050B/2767